Claimed by her Cougar

Felicity Heaton

COUGAR CREEK MATES SERIES

Claimed by her Cougar
Captured by her Cougar (Coming August 18th 2018)
Courted by her Cougar (Coming September 8th 2018)
Craved by her Cougar (Coming September 29th 2018)

Cougar Creek Mates is set in the same world as the Eternal Mates Series

ETERNAL MATES SERIES

Kissed by a Dark Prince
Claimed by a Demon King
Tempted by a Rogue Prince
Hunted by a Jaguar
Craved by an Alpha
Bitten by a Hellcat
Taken by a Dragon
Marked by an Assassin
Possessed by a Dark Warrior
Awakened by a Demoness
Haunted by the King of Death
Turned by a Tiger
Tamed by a Tiger
Treasured by a Tiger
Unchained by a Forbidden Love

Find out more at: www.felicityheaton.com

CHAPTER 1

In the tranquil morning air, a deer called out, the sound echoing around the mountains sheltering the peaceful verdant valley.

Rath stilled, froze right down to his breathing as his ears twitched and he cocked his head, the instinct to hunt that animal sweeping through him and tugging at his cougar side. When the call didn't come again, he exhaled slowly, releasing his breath and using the action to centre himself, and looked to his left, out of the window that formed a triangle on the gable end of his log cabin, nestled beneath the two sides of the pitched roof where it hung out over the deck below to provide cover.

Mist swirled above the sweeping bend of the river that formed a barrier between him and the thick forest that blanketed the other side, where his senses had pinpointed the deer, among other creatures stirring in the early morning as darkness began to give way to light. The tendrils of fog crept over the stony bank of the river in places, crawling across the grass and into the pines that flanked the open ground on his side of the creek, reaching the deck of the cabin nearest it.

His was too distant, close to two hundred metres from the river across the grass. It was rare for the spring morning mists to reach his home, happened only once or twice a season, the sun too swift to rise and burn them away before they could creep that far up the sloping green.

Rath lingered and let the beauty of the scene wash over him, savouring the peace because it would be shattered soon.

Gods, he wanted his instincts as an unmated male cougar to be wrong, but they hadn't been yet.

This year, there would be a gathering.

He grabbed his long-sleeved cream t-shirt from the banister at the front of the loft bedroom and tugged it on, following it with a thick dark green fleece that had a zip that reached the centre of his chest. He pulled his faded jeans on and buttoned them as he descended the wooden steps to the ground floor of the cabin. It was small, had only two rooms on the lower level—an open plan kitchen and living room, and an enclosed bathroom— but it was more than big enough for him.

A huff burst from his lips when he saw the fire in the log burner was low. No wonder it was so damned cold this morning. He moved around the worn beige couch and crouched before it, opened the door and tossed another log on, and warmed his hands as he waited for it to catch. When the fire was blazing again and the chill of morning was off his hands, he yawned and latched the door, and rose back onto his feet.

Gods, he needed coffee.

Rath scrubbed a hand over the two-days' growth on his face, thought about shaving and then shrugged it off. He was going to be out all day again, repairing the cabin by the river and clearing up a few more odd jobs he needed to complete around the settlement at the other dozen or so cabins spread throughout the trees on his side of the river. A little insulation on his face wasn't a bad thing.

Winter had loosened its grip on Cougar Creek, but the mornings and evenings were still chilly, the air holding a bitter bite that was slow to go as the sun struggled to heat the land and quick to return once darkness fell again.

He had been working non-stop since the snowmelt, when that damned feeling had stirred in his gut and he had found himself pacing the porch, scenting the air, hungry for a female he didn't want and didn't need.

Wasn't going to chase.

Gatherings meant one thing for him and his brothers—patrolling the area, acting as a security force to keep the community safe when they were together and in danger of attracting attention.

They also acted as a security force within the pride too, breaking up any fights that weren't over a female.

Cougars were solitary, so things always got tense when the entire pride gathered in the small village of cabins. The lodges were scattered throughout the broad band of forest that hugged the mountain behind him and the river before him, with enough space between them to keep everyone calm, but there were always a few males too riled up by the season and the reason they were at the village, and fights always broke out.

Last time a gathering had happened, he had personally intervened in more than a dozen brawls, tearing the two opponents off each other and confining them to their cabins for a day or two as punishment.

His three younger brothers weren't as diplomatic. Storm in particular loved getting stuck into a fight, bashing heads and drawing blood, giving the two males a taste of his strength.

Storm hated being in charge of overseeing the gathering, would prefer to be in the thick of it, fighting and fucking, but it was tradition for their bloodline now, and that meant his brother was confined to the side lines with the rest of them.

Personally, Rath wasn't interested in the gathering at all, would rather it never happened, or at least happened elsewhere, somewhere far away from Cougar Creek.

He didn't need females invading his territory.

Wasn't interested in the silent, or sometimes not so silent, invitations they issued to him.

He would leave the job of satisfying them to the other males who would follow their instincts back to the pride village, forgoing their solitary life for a few weeks to wait for the females to come and to fight for dominance and the right to be the one who would ease her needing.

Hell, some of them would even mate.

Rath paused at the kitchen counter in front of the picture window, staring out of it at the lush grass and the valley beyond it, and the snow-capped mountains that rose in the distance, seeing a different time, one close to fifty years ago now.

When he had found a mate of his own.

One who had been ripped from him.

He shoved her out of his thoughts and focused on his morning ritual, reaching for the cafetiere and setting it down on the polished wooden counter, spooning coffee grounds into the bottom of it and then grabbing the steel kettle. He set it on the stove, stooped and grabbed the white plastic water container and growled.

It was empty.

Shit.

He had meant to fill it last night before heading to bed, but had been so tired after finishing the repairs to the inside of the cabin nearest the river, one of a couple that had been damaged by a winter storm, that he had passed out on the couch.

A cabin he would have to work on again today, getting the roof repaired, because he was running out of time.

3

The family who owned it had sent word that they would be arriving soon.

The letter he had picked up on a supply run to the nearest settlement had contained more than just news of their imminent arrival though.

It had contained a request for him to personally court the female who would be coming, one who had recently reached her one hundredth year and matured.

He wasn't interested and he would make that clear when the party arrived, would have sent them a damned reply already if they had chosen to email him rather than sending a letter. A flat refusal wouldn't appease this particular family, would only see them trying to convince him, so he would use his position as pride protector as a shield to get them to change their mind, telling them he couldn't participate.

The only thing he wanted to take care of were the cabins.

He stuffed his feet into his black boots, grabbed the empty water can and a metal pail, and zipped up his fleece before opening the door and bracing himself. Damn, it was cold. He needed water, and then coffee, lots of coffee, before he could brave the weather and start work on the roof of the cabin.

His strides were quick at first, carrying him off the raised deck and down the steps to the grass, but they slowed as he looked at the valley, at his home, breathed in the crisp air and absorbed the silence, falling back into savouring it again, clinging to these last remnants of quiet before the storm hit.

Literally.

Things always got crazy when his brothers descended on him all at once, returning from the cities to annoy him for weeks on end, stomping all over his territory and invading his space.

His second youngest brother, Storm, always lived up to his name, and he was due to return soon, before the others and before the males came for the gathering, having drawn the short straw to help him prepare all the cabins, opening them up and airing them out, and getting any last minute repairs completed.

A smile tugged at his lips. It would be good to see him though. It had been more than a year since Storm had hit the creek, his work keeping him away. Rath appreciated the extra funds rolling in from his direction though, so he wasn't going to complain when he saw him. Everyone who owned a cabin at the creek donated to running the village, paying Rath a small wage that covered whatever food and supplies he had to buy and couldn't just hunt or gather.

He glanced at the single storey log cabin nestled beneath the trees to his left and groaned as he saw the state of the right hand side of the pitched roof. He was going to be up there for hours, repairing and replacing all those shingles. Still, he would have one heck of a view.

Rath looked to his right, at the river and the mist that danced above it, swirling in places as the breeze stirred it. Birdsong filled the air, the sound a melody he always loved hearing, and the sun cast a golden glow over the fog as it rose, and turned the snow on the peaks amber too. The sky beyond them was clear today, threaded with only fingers of clouds that burned gold in the sunrise.

Fuck, it was beautiful.

The bite in the air felt good in his lungs, invigorating him.

He looked back at the cabin, at the damage that had been done to the roof when the lodgepole pines that sheltered it had shed snow on it, the sudden impact breaking a whole area of old shingles and one of the roof trusses. The square window on that side of the gable end had a crack in it and would need repairing too, but he would have to patch it up for now, until he could get some glass in. He was sure the family would understand he had prioritised the roof and replacing the old rotten deck planks, and that other cabins had needed his attention so he hadn't been able to get new glass.

The cabin was larger than his own, formed an L shape in the woods, branching off to the left of the front of the cabin, around the tallest lodgepole pine, and the ceiling was vaulted inside, left open above the rooms.

It added a feeling of space, but Rath preferred having his bedroom in the loft, making use of the roof area.

Plus, he had a fantastic view of the valley from his bed.

He twisted the cap off the white water container and stuck it in his back pocket as he approached the river. When he hit the pebbled bank, he set the container down and bent to scoop water into the pail.

He paused.

His ears twitched.

The birds fell silent.

His instincts rose to the fore, heightening his senses, and he swept them around him, searching for the source of the disturbance he had felt. Something was out there. It was probably just one of the local animals on the other side of the river, stepping out of cover to scare the birds. With the mist, he couldn't see the bank on that side, and it had him twitchy, his cougar instincts putting him on high alert.

Only one thing in the valley could harm him, and possibly kill him, and the bear shifters tended to keep to themselves and avoid the creek.

Whatever had just wandered into his territory was just an animal, not a threat to him.

Still, he tipped his head back and drew air over his teeth, scenting it to see what he was dealing with.

Rath stilled as he didn't scent an animal.

He smelled a human.

A floral note, tinged with sweat. Probably a hiker, but he was damned if a human was going to encroach on his territory.

He set the pail down beside the container as he rose onto his feet in one fluid motion. He tracked the scent through the mist, following it along the bank to the right of the clearing. It grew stronger as he reached the trees, and he slowed his breathing and moved stealthily through the fog, his acute senses charting the route ahead of him. His muscles coiled as he focused, his senses heightening further, and he assessed the danger and the human he could now feel ahead of him, barely twenty metres away.

They were still on his senses.

Stalking something?

He slowed his movements, each step careful and silent, so he didn't alert them, just in case it was a hunter strayed into his territory.

His vision sharpened, allowing him to see the human before it could see him through the mist, giving him the upper hand.

Rath stilled again.

It wasn't a male.

It was a female.

A curvy brunette who looked as stunned as he felt as the mist cleared between them and she lifted her head and blinked at him.

She wasn't a hunter either.

She had been shooting, but it wasn't a gun she had aimed at him.

It was a camera.

CHAPTER 2

If the tip she had received turned out to be nothing, Ivy was going to kill the person who had given it to her. She rubbed her hands together, struggling to keep the chill off her numbed fingers as she made her way through the thick coniferous woods, following a faint path that she hoped would lead her down to the river she had heard almost a mile back. She paused and checked her position on her GPS.

She was getting close to the coordinates she had been given now, and not even the freezing morning temperatures, or the chilly night camping that had seen her awake more than asleep, listening tensely to every noise in the darkness, could dampen her excitement.

Black bears.

If she could get some photographs of a mother with cubs in undisturbed habitat, it would be incredible, perfect for her series on Canadian bears, an idea she had hit on last year when trying to shatter a creative wall that had left her close to giving up photography altogether.

Yasmin had talked her through it, always the voice of reason and support, convincing her not to give up just yet and to think of a project that could stir her passion again.

Ivy was glad that she had listened and had decided to try a series on bears, because some of the photos she had taken of grizzlies in the fall had restored her faith and now she had found the energy she had been missing, the enthusiasm she had always had for photography.

It wasn't her work. It was her passion.

One she couldn't believe she had almost given up on now that she was back in the saddle.

She carefully picked a path over the roots of the spruces and pines that towered above her, half of her focus on the world around her and half of it on the project.

If things went well with the black bears, maybe she could head over to the coast and find some spirit bears. It would be more of a challenge, but she had done her research and there was a place that was off the beaten trail, just like this one. No tourist groups to disturb her work or get in the way. Just unspoilt and untamed nature at its finest. She could picture the photographs now, just as she could see the ones she could get in her current location, and another bubble of excitement burst inside her, bringing a smile to her lips.

She could do it if her funding held.

Ivy didn't want to think about that, not when what had happened with one of her sponsors had sent her into her creative depression in the first place.

She adjusted the straps of her backpack, one that he had bought her.

One she had wanted to ditch but getting a bag of this calibre, one that could safely store all her equipment, some clothing and food, and her camping gear, was expensive, and she had never been one to do something as frivolous as throwing away a perfectly good bag and buying a replacement.

Her budget was stretched tight enough as it was.

She was damned if she was going to risk running out of money just to spite a man who didn't give a damn about her.

Ivy paused and listened, searching for the sound of the river through the patches of birdsong. Nothing. She pushed onwards, heaving a sigh as her feet started to ache in her boots. She must have walked a few miles already, had started out from her camping spot at first light, as soon as she had been able to walk without needing a flashlight.

It was growing lighter now.

Ahead of her, the trees thinned, and she peered through them. Golden light cast shadows, telling her there was an opening of some sort in that direction.

She quickened her pace, the thought of standing in the weak sunlight and letting it warm her driving her more than the thought the river might be there. She needed to warm up or her brain was going to freeze. She should have found her gloves in her pack this morning, and maybe a hat, something to keep the chill off so it wasn't such a distraction, but she had been so excited by the thought of finding black bears in this pristine wilderness that she had rushed to keep moving towards the location she had been given.

An animal called in the distance and she stilled, her head whipping in all directions, pulse jacking up as she listened hard, trying to figure out where the sound had come from, and what had made it.

A deer broke cover just a few metres ahead of her and she almost shrieked as she jumped and stumbled back a step. The heel of her hiking boot caught on a root and threatened to send her down, and she staggered as she fought to maintain her balance so she didn't land on her backside, and her pack.

The animal glanced her way, called again and bounded into the trees to her right as she grabbed the trunk of the pine to stop herself from falling and breathed hard and fast, her heart hammering as adrenaline flooded her veins, leaving her trembling.

When the sound of its footfalls disappeared, and the birds began singing again, she breathed a little easier, focused on each one she pulled down into her lungs to steady her racing heart as she sagged against the tree.

Damn, being so deep in the woods was making her jittery.

She wasn't sure she had ever ventured so far into the wilderness before, and she hadn't realised it would put her so on edge, afraid of every noise she heard. She had been so caught up in the fact the person she had spoken to at a bar in Golden, deep in the heart of the Canadian Rockies, had told her he had seen a lot of bears in this valley in the past that she hadn't really thought about how remote it was.

Or how alone she was.

Normally when she headed into the wilder places in the world, she had a guide with her.

This time, she was flying solo.

Looking for bears.

Damn, she hoped she hadn't made a terrible mistake by trekking into the middle of nowhere and wasn't about to meet a grisly end.

Pun intended.

Ivy looked back over her shoulder as she palmed the bear spray hanging from her belt of her brown trousers, using the feel of it to calm her nerves. If she trekked all day, she could probably make it back to her Jeep where she had parked it at the end of a logging track. It would be dark when she got there, but she could sleep in the safety of the vehicle and drive at first light.

She glanced at the forest around her, and shook her head, causing her ponytail to sway across the shoulders of her beige weatherproof jacket.

No. She had to keep going forwards, wouldn't be able to live with herself if she didn't do this. It would always play on her mind, tormenting her with the fact she had given up when she might have been able to get award-winning photographs of bears.

When she scanned the woods again, and spotted mist creeping through the trees below her to her right, her feet took the decision out of her hands. She marched down the slope, winding through the broad trunks of the ancient trees, and slowed as she left them behind.

The river.

It was eerily silent as it stretched before her, shallow and broad, rippling over rocks.

She stared at the dense dark green woods on the other side and the mountains that speared the azure sky beyond them, the cragged peaks still laced with snow.

The beauty of it hit her hard, had her standing still and taking it in as she swept her gaze across the scenery, to her left towards where the sun was rising, not quite visible beyond a dip in the mountains.

She wasn't sure she had ever been anywhere that felt so tranquil.

Where she felt miles from civilisation.

It was breathtaking.

A smile crept onto her lips. The trek and the terrifying night sleeping in a flimsy tent had been worth it just to see this.

She followed the rocky bank of the river, letting it lead her now, forgetting her GPS, sure this was the spot the old man had told her about, and that she would get the photographs of bears that she wanted here, if she had a little patience.

And damn, they were going to be amazing.

She could feel it as a shiver over her skin, a sweep of prickles that stirred her excitement to a whole new level and had her looking at all the angles, seeking just the right one to make a composition that would blow the world away.

She found it as she rounded a bend in the river and the trees hugging the bank eased away from it, allowing the scenery to open up.

It was perfect.

Incredible.

The shallow river rippled over rocks, flowing swiftly around the bend, and trees enclosed it on both sides. The mountains embraced those trees, rising high into the sky. Yes, this was the place. She was going to get the shots she wanted here, she was sure of it.

As the sun broke the horizon above the mountains, and mist swirled across the river, she reached for her camera. She had to photograph it. It was too beautiful to let it slip through her grasp. She pulled her backpack off, set it down on the bank near the trees and unzipped it, taking out her camera. She fixed a wide-angle lens on it, one that would give her enough field of view to really capture the beauty of the valley but could zoom to give her a close up if a bear appeared, and positioned herself.

Ivy snapped a picture and looked down at the screen of her Nikon, smiled at the shot, adjusted her settings, and lifted her camera to take another. As she swept it across the scenery, looking for the best composition, she imagined a black bear emerging from the haze and how perfect it would be. It was a magical scene as the sun rose and mist hung just above the rippling water, and it would only be made even more magical by a bear.

She took a handful of photographs, the changing light as the sun rose leading her to take another and then another, documenting the splendour of the scene as it subtly shifted.

She had never seen anything so beautiful.

So breathtaking.

She swung her camera left, towards the side of the river she was on, wanting to capture a shot of it with the glacier in the distance and the sun rising above it.

A shape loomed in the mist, disturbing it, and her heart lodged in her throat, a thrill chasing through her as she pressed down on the shutter release, sure it was a bear.

But as the mist parted, it wasn't a bear that emerged.

It was a man.

A mountain of one.

He moved towards her with a predator's gait, prowling through the mist that tried to cling to his long powerful jeans-clad legs and the cuffs of his worn dark green fleece, the sun rising behind him casting golden highlights in his thick dark hair. His square jaw, shadowed by stubble, tensed and his stony grey eyes darkened as they narrowed on her.

It took Ivy a moment to realise he was talking to her.

"You're trespassing." His gravelly deep voice rolled over her, a growl that suited his appearance.

He looked more dangerous than the wild animals in these parts.

A hunter?

She wasn't sure how she was trespassing. As far as she knew, no one owned the land she was on, and she had done her research to make sure she didn't accidentally do exactly what he was accusing her of doing.

He lowered his steely grey eyes and his handsome face twisted in a savage expression as they landed on her camera.

"Hand it over." He held his right hand out to her.

Ivy clutched her camera to her chest. Like hell she was handing it over to him. It had cost her thousands of dollars.

"No." She eased back a step and glanced at her backpack where it sat on the bank a few metres behind her, and then at the man.

He looked fit, and as if he belonged in this wild world, and she wasn't sure she would make it more than a few metres if she tried to run. He would easily catch her. Her heart pounded at that, and she wasn't sure whether it was out of fear or something else.

Something she was not going to examine closely.

The bear spray on her belt suddenly felt heavy, and she was tempted to use it on him, would if it came to it, even though it was against the law. Diplomacy was always the first weapon she reached for in situations like this though, one that often had the desired effect. He wasn't the first man to attempt to block her path, and he wouldn't be the last.

He continued to scowl at her camera. "Why are you here?"

"I'm photographing bears." She debated showing him the pictures in the hope it would convince him that she wasn't a threat, but hit two snags.

He would have to get close to her in order to see them, meaning he could easily snatch her camera or her, and she had put a fresh memory card in the camera last night, not wanting to have to scramble for a new one if she ran out of space when photographing bears.

He didn't look as if he believed her.

Ivy turned towards her bag, heart slamming as she decided to risk it and find the memory card she had with photos on it.

The man was behind her in an instant, closing the distance so swiftly that it tore a shocked gasp from her lips as his left hand locked around her right wrist.

She stumbled as he pulled her towards her backpack and twisted her arm in his hand, trying to break free.

The bastard had a grip like iron.

She clutched her camera with her left hand and struggled harder, adrenaline flooding her veins to push her to fight for her freedom as her blood rushed, heart thundering in her throat. "Get off me."

Screw diplomacy.

Ivy released her camera and seized her bear spray in trembling fingers, yanking it from her belt and aiming it at him. He launched his other hand towards her and snatched the canister before she could depress the trigger, scowled at it and then at her, and started pulling her along again.

"You need to answer some questions." The dark note in his voice rang warning bells in her head and she kicked him in the shin, sure he would release her.

He just glared at her and kept dragging her along. When she tripped on a rock, he pulled on her arm, raising his above his head so quickly she avoided faceplanting on the ground. A bastard with a grip of iron and the reflexes of a cat.

She refused to thank him, shot him a scowl when he looked as if he was expecting one, and found her footing again, a strange calmness coming over her as she checked her Nikon to make sure she hadn't scuffed it on the rocks. As soon as she saw it was fine, that odd sense of calm dissipated, her situation flooding back in to shake her all over again.

The man grabbed her backpack, slung it over his shoulder and marched her along the shore, ignoring her struggles as she tried to prise his hand off her, working her fingers under his in an attempt to loosen them.

They didn't budge.

Bastard.

He was big, stood close to a foot taller than her and his shoulders were twice as broad as hers. His dark green fleece hugged his physique to mock her with his apparent strength. It wasn't going to deter her. Even the biggest men had a weakness, and she would find his.

Her eyes widened, fighting him forgotten as a clearing came into view, a stretch of grass that spanned at least a hundred metres along the river and ran maybe twice that back towards the mountain. In among the trees, hidden beneath their evergreen canopies, cabins nestled, each of them a different shape and size.

She hadn't seen any of them in the aerial shots of the valley, had figured the man for a camper, but it looked as if he lived here.

In the middle of nowhere.

"Are you a hunter?" She stared at the back of his head.

He glared over his wide shoulders at her. "No… and I don't tolerate hunters here either."

"I'm not a hunter." She huffed when he still looked as if he didn't believe her. "I'll show you proof if you let me go!"

This time, when she twisted free of his grip, he released her, the suddenness of it sending her off balance, so she had to plant her foot out to stop herself from falling over. For a moment, she thought he had released her so she could show him her photographs, but then he stooped, grabbed a silver pail and filled it in the river. He poured it into a white container, and followed it with two more scoops, glared at the container and the small amount of water in it, and then at her, as if it was her fault he was collecting so little.

She realised it was when he grabbed her arm again, pulling her up the grassy slope.

"I thought we were done with the caveman act." She kicked him in the back of the leg and must have caught him in a sweet spot because his left leg buckled, sending him down onto one knee.

And jerking her with him.

She squeaked as she hit the grass, twisting just in time to make sure her shoulder took the blow and not her camera.

He shoved her arm away from him, his expression stormy as he pushed back onto his feet, and checked his damned water, holding it up and looking a hell of a lot relieved when he saw he hadn't spilled it. He pulled a cap from the back pocket of his jeans, revealing a heck of a fine backside as he lifted the hem of his green fleece, and screwed it onto the canister.

This time when he started moving, he didn't grab her and drag her with him. Score one for her.

He scored a point of his own when he said without looking back at her, "I'm making coffee, and I'm feeling generous today. If you want some, and a chance to explain what you're doing on my land, come with me. If you don't, get the fuck off my property before I drive you off it."

Charming.

But the thought of a hot drink, and the sight of smoke curling lazily from the metal chimney on the roof of the log cabin he was heading towards, had her picking herself up, grabbing her bag and following him.

And not only because she wanted to warm up.

She had the feeling that if she could just convince him that she wasn't here for any nefarious reason, he would let her stay and photograph the bears.

She looked back at the river, and the mist that still swirled above it, eager to return to it in case any bears came to it while it looked so magical.

He disappeared into the cabin.

Ivy forced herself to follow him, nerves rising again as she approached the small building. A voice whispered not to go into it, that he was luring her in there for nefarious reasons of his own and that she should just leave now before it was too late.

He had been rough with her, forceful.

She had no reason to trust him, to believe he wouldn't hurt her or abuse her.

He appeared in the window to the right of the open door, paused at his work and looked up at her, his grey eyes looking more blue in the light. His dark eyebrows drew down and he moved, disappearing from view for a heartbeat before he appeared in the doorway.

"Have a seat out here if it will make you feel more at ease." His bass voice curled around her, a hint of warmth in it now, and in his eyes too as he gazed at her, his irises appearing more gold than grey now.

A trick of the light?

She eyed the two wooden chairs on the deck, and then peered into his cabin as he moved back into it, at the log burner against the left wall of it. It was warmer in there, but the thought of going inside had her nerves rising so she settled herself on the chair below the window and put her pack down by her feet.

Her focus strayed to the river as she waited, and it was hard to resist snapping a few shots of the valley as the sun rose higher. The way he had reacted to her photographing the valley had her holding off though, afraid that if she dared to take any more pictures that he would kick her out and her chance to photograph the bears she was sure came to the area would be lost.

He emerged from the cabin to her right and set a chipped white mug down on the table beside her. The coffee was black, and she preferred hers white, but she was damned if she was going to mention it. Steam rose off it, luring her in with the promise of warmth, and she grabbed it and lifted it to her lips, and breathed in the aroma.

A contented sigh swept through her.

While he lacked milk and manners, he had good taste in coffee, clearly made it using grounds and not instant granules.

She would have thanked him if he hadn't chosen that moment to speak.

"So, you have your coffee, where's my proof?" He remained standing, a glowering tower of muscle and menace, his eyes dark and stormy again as he fixed her with a hard look and nursed his own cup of coffee.

Clearly the caffeine hadn't improved his manners.

She reluctantly set her mug down, rifled through her backpack and found her stash of memory cards. She inserted one in her camera, found it was blank, and tried another, growing increasingly aware of the man where he stood over her, waiting.

"I have proof," she muttered, sure he was convinced otherwise by now.

Her heart did a flip in her chest when the camera revealed pictures on the card she had inserted, and she quickly flicked through them, her hands shaking as she hunted for the ones she had taken last fall. There were a lot of eagles, and some deer, and other animals, but no bears. Damn it. She wiped the back of her hand across her brow, clearing the sweat gathering on it as she stewed under his fierce scrutiny, and kept skimming through the photographs.

Relief crashed over her when she found the shots, and she looked up the height of him, into eyes that were definitely more gold than grey now. "No stealing my camera."

He arched an eyebrow at that, and how fiercely she clutched it to her, and even sighed as she placed the strap back around her neck so he couldn't easily grab it off her.

Of course, she hadn't considered something important when she had chosen to protect her camera by placing the strap around her neck.

The fact he would have to get close to her to see the pictures on the screen.

When he hunkered down beside her, his big body crowding her and making her feel small despite her generous curves, and his masculine earthy scent and heat flowing over her, she swallowed hard and did her damnedest to ignore the way it lit her up inside, warmed her better than any fire could have.

He prodded the screen. "That's a grizzly."

Duh.

The huge brown bear was unmistakable with its long nose and hump on its back above its front legs.

"I took it around a hundred miles from here last fall. It's part of a series I'm shooting about Canadian bears." She wiped the smudge from his finger from the screen, trying not to huff as she did it, using it as something to focus on other than how near he was to her and the way her blood was turning to molten fire in her veins, burning hotter the longer he remained hunkered down beside her.

She flicked to the next picture, and then the next, until he had seen all of them and she was sure he would move away again.

She lifted her eyes at the same time as he did and stilled as they locked, that heat rolling through her rapidly reaching boiling point.

Hell, he was closer than she had realised, so close she could pick out flecks of gold and blue against the stony grey in his irises and that the dark stubble coating his square jaw concealed a slight dip in the centre of his chin.

He stared at her, his pupils slowly dilating, a hint of blue-green emerging around them as they devoured the grey. The tension in the air thickened, the heat like an inferno now as she lost herself in his eyes, couldn't shake herself out of whatever trance he had placed her in.

Or maybe it was a trance that had come over them both, because he shook his head and a flicker of a frown caused his eyebrows to dip, and then he eased back on his haunches.

He cleared his throat and the banked heat in his eyes was devoured by a glacial abyss. "That proves nothing. Hunters often take pictures during recon missions to new areas, so their friends can see proof there are bears."

Good grief, he had to be the least trusting person she had ever met. It was infuriating.

"Well, it's all I have. My laptop is back in my Jeep and even then I could only show you more pictures and some official documents, and I'm guessing you want to see something like my website or awards or maybe my damned passport and a certificate that states in big letters that I'm not a hunter!"

Her outburst didn't even make him flinch.

He just regarded her coolly for a few seconds before pushing onto his feet, setting his mug down beside hers, and striding back into his cabin.

What the hell was he up to now?

She snagged her coffee and sipped it, trying to get her nerves back under control as her heart jittered around in her chest. He was being unreasonable. She had given him all the proof she could. When he came back, she was just going to ask him whether or not he was going to let her stay on his land to photograph the bears.

She set her mug back down and focused on switching the memory cards in her camera again, and looked at the pictures she had taken.

Including a shot of him.

Hell, he fitted right into his wild surroundings, as rugged as the mountains and alluring as the big cats that roamed them.

The man emerged from the cabin again, and she switched off her camera and opened her mouth and then snapped it shut again, her eyebrows drawing down as she spotted the silver laptop he carried. He leaned against the railing that ran around the deck, his back to the valley, opened the computer and looked down at the screen as it lit up, holding the laptop in his left hand, resting against his thighs.

The light from it made his eyes look blue again, and she found herself staring up at them, wondering how they changed depending on the light or the angle she was at to him. She had never noticed anyone else's eyes do that. Maybe it was the flecks of colours in them catching the light, creating the illusion they had changed colour.

Her eyebrows rose.

Did her eyes change like his?

Hers were hazel, flecked with gold. Maybe they appeared more gold at times to people.

His gaze shifted to her, he twisted the laptop towards her and jerked his chin. "Show me this website of yours."

She took the laptop, shifted her camera to one side so it didn't get in the way, and settled it on her lap. In the corner of the screen, the computer showed a strong internet connection. Not surprising, although it probably would have shocked most people. She hadn't missed the row of solar panels he had peeking out from beneath the trees to her right. If he was generating his own electricity, it stood to reason he had a few modern conveniences like satellite internet.

She typed in the address of her website and handed the computer back to him, her gaze drifting to the river as he took it from her. She wanted to be there, with her camera poised, waiting for a bear to show up. The sun was creeping higher now, and the mist was growing thinner. It would be gone before long, and so would the opportunity to get the picture she had envisaged.

"Ivy Wentworth," he drawled, voice so smooth and deep that warmth curled through her in response, and she had to shake her head to push out that image of him stalking towards her through the mist, his eyes locked on her, intense and focused.

"That's me." She swallowed to wet her dry throat, reminded herself that she wasn't looking for a man, had been burned one time too many, and lifted her eyes from the river to him.

He glanced at her, and then frowned back at the screen, tapping the tracking pad. He was silent for so long that she had half a mind to ask whether she could at least go back to the river and look for bears while he pored over her life's work.

He finally huffed, snapped the laptop closed and regarded her with a cool gaze that gave nothing away.

"Satisfied now?" She tipped her chin up and held his gaze, refusing to let him fluster her as he stared at her in silence.

He hiked his wide shoulders. "You seem legit... and not a hunter."

The dark way he said that left her feeling it was a good thing for her, that he was being positively polite compared with how he would have been treating her if she had turned out to be a hunter.

"So am I still being kicked off your land?" Land she wasn't sure he owned or had any right to kick her off of anyway.

He placed the laptop down on the other chair, resumed his position against the railing, resting his backside against it, and held his right hand out to her.

"I want to see the pictures you took today."

Ivy held back her sigh, switched her camera on again, and angled it towards him. He stooped beside her, that heat curling around her again, making it difficult to focus on the fact he had been nothing but a bastard to her. She'd had her fair share of bastards and was done with them. Yasmin was right about the fact they didn't deserve her.

She flicked through the pictures, frowned at him when he tried to touch the screen again and moved it away from him, fielding a black look from him that lasted only a second before he looked back down at the screen.

And his entire face darkened.

"Delete that." His voice was a low growl in her ear.

She looked down at the photograph. One of him. Clearly he didn't like being photographed. She shifted her thumb to the delete button and paused with it hovering over it, her eyes on the screen and the image of him emerging from the mist. Damn, he had looked magnificent.

It was a shame he had turned out to be as growly as the grizzlies in these parts.

He pressed her thumb down on the button, and she scowled at him for taking the decision out of her hands. When he saw there were other pictures of him, he seized the camera and tugged it towards him, and glared at it as he deleted them.

Every single one of them.

Erasing himself from history?

Maybe the solitude had gone to his head and he had gone a little crazy.

A chill swept down her spine.

Or maybe there was a reason he was hiding out here in the wilderness and got jumpy when a stranger strolled onto his perceived property.

She slowly, cautiously took the camera from him, and he rose back onto his feet to tower over her, a six-six wall that looked just as formidable now as he had when he had been dragging her along the riverbank.

Her heart pounded as their eyes met, heat blooming unbidden in her blood as his narrowed on hers and darkened with something she couldn't call anger this time.

She wanted to look away, but held his gaze, breathed through the strange surge of sensation that went through her and focused on the reason she was here, using it to shut down the unruly part of herself that kept responding to him in a highly inappropriate, and unsettling, way.

"So are there bears here?" Her voice sounded small, fragile, weak in her ears.

He nodded and averted his eyes, fixing them on the river to his right. She had the damnedest feeling he was avoiding her.

Maybe he had been burned too.

Maybe that was the reason he was out here, alone in the middle of nowhere.

"Can I wait and see if I can get a picture of them? Just a few shots. That's all I need."

His stony eyes landed on her again. "No. I want you gone now."

Damn him. She wasn't going to go down without a fight, not now she knew there were bears here.

"Fine, I'll go further up the valley."

He met those words with a black look and bit out, "No, you won't. It's dangerous beyond this point."

"Do you own that land too?" She felt sure she was getting somewhere now, used the tiny sliver of compassion and concern he had revealed to her to her advantage. When he shook his head, she shrugged. "So you have no way of stopping me going up that way. I'll be off your land."

He folded his thick arms across his broad chest and glared down at her, his jaw muscles popping beneath his dark scruff. He had done enough intimidating her for one day. She was done with it.

"I either go up the valley or photograph the bears here. Your choice." She bit back her smile when his expression darkened further and he looked as if he was chewing on a wasp.

"I can't let you go up the valley." His grey eyes looked more gold again as he stared into hers, his pupils dilating to darken them. "You can stay here for the morning, but I want you gone in the afternoon."

She smiled up at him. Score another one for her.

He looked away from her, frowning at the river, and when his eyes slid back to her, they were definitely more gold than grey, sent a shiver through her as they met hers and had that banked heat threatening to burst into wildfire as he spoke, his deep voice rolling over her, through her, lighting her up in a dangerous way.

"But I'm not letting you out of my sight."

CHAPTER 3

Rath wasn't sure what had possessed him, why he had laid down the law and made it clear that he would be escorting Little Miss Ivy wherever she went on his property.

It had been instinct, but he wasn't sure whether it had stemmed from a desire to protect the secrets of his home and his kin, or a desire to protect her.

Her careless talk of heading up river into the valley had provoked a fierce reaction from his cougar side, had made him instantly restless, stoked by an urge to force her to stay within the boundaries of his territory.

Where she would be safe.

He shoved away from the railing around his deck before he could even consider thinking about the reason why he wanted to protect her, snagged his mug and tossed the cold coffee onto the grass, and then strode into his cabin. He poured another mug, lifted it to his lips and drank it while looking at the river. It was only a few hours. He could work on the cabin by the river after she was gone.

His eyes dropped to her, and he watched her as she fiddled with the camera she had protected as if it was her damned baby rather than a piece of soulless machinery.

Maybe not soulless.

Her photographs had been good, and the ones on her website had been impressive too. She had talent.

He swigged his coffee, savouring the warmth of it and the buzz as the caffeine instantly hit him. Fuck, he had needed that.

She moved again, rubbing her wrist this time, and he looked away when she pulled the sleeve of her beige jacket back to reveal a dark mark on her arm, something twisting in his chest at the sight of it.

He hadn't meant to be a dick. It just came with the territory. It was his job to keep Cougar Creek secret from the world, protected. She hadn't been the first human to wander into the creek, but she was the first he was going to let leave.

The other humans that had all strayed onto his land had been hunting, and some of them had been taking photographs.

He and his kin had realised it was better to kill any suspicious humans after they had allowed one to leave and they had turned out to be a scouting party for a mortal hunter organisation bent on eradicating non-humans.

Archangel.

The bastards had paid for their attempt to murder his entire pride, but they had forced them to move the entire community to a new location, one he intended to keep safe.

Ivy pushed onto her feet, snagging his focus again as she slipped her arm through the strap of her camera, so it sat across her chest and the camera hung at her right hip, and smoothed rogue strands of her rich brown hair back into her ponytail. She brushed her dark brown trekking trousers down, frowning as she spotted the mud all around her ankles, and stooped, giving him a hell of a view of her round backside as she tucked her trousers into the tops of her walking boots.

Rath dragged his eyes away from her and growled at himself.

He stomped out onto the deck as his mood soured for some godsdamned reason and didn't look at her as he hit the grass and growled, "Keep up."

"Manners much?" she muttered, his sensitive hearing easily picking up her soft voice.

He glared at the grass, a need to turn and tell her that he had manners pounding through him, but she would only ask where they were, and he didn't have an answer for that question. He wasn't sure where they had gone.

They had disappeared the moment he had set eyes on her by the river, the second she had lowered her camera and her eyes had met his, and something had happened. He just wasn't sure what that something was. It had him tied in knots, snapping at her when he felt guilty about it a split-second later, unsure what the fuck was wrong with him.

He led her to the river, positioned himself on a log beneath a tree on the right side of the grassy area, and leaned back against the broad trunk of the pine.

Watching her.

She lifted the camera to her face and swung it in all directions, diligently keeping it away from him. The morning mist curled playfully around her boots as she did whatever the fuck she was doing. He had never taken a picture in his life, had no clue what she was looking for through the lens. Whatever it was, she seemed to find it when she moved to the other side of the grass, to the trees near the cabin there, and hunkered down, going incredibly still.

Rath tried to do the same, but his right leg twitched and he tapped his fingers on his knee as he watched her.

Couldn't keep his damned eyes off her.

She stayed perfectly still for close to an hour, and then stood and lowered the camera to her hip. She raised her arms above her head and stretched, pushing her breasts outwards, pulling her thick jacket tight across them.

His cougar side growled at the vision of her, growing restless as he studied her, and he tapped his knee harder. When she turned his way, lowering her arms, he averted his gaze, locking it on the river. The sun was rising higher, clearing the mist now. He basked in it, letting the warmth wash over him and soak into his dark clothing, and distract him from her as it roused his love of lazing in the sunshine.

It wouldn't be long before summer rolled in.

Gods, the thought of long days spent stretched out in the sunshine had him aching for it to roll around quicker.

He wouldn't say no to skipping spring, didn't need the damned headache of a gathering wrecking his year.

"It's beautiful here." Ivy's soft voice coming from close to him had him whipping his head towards her. She smiled down at him. "I didn't mean to startle you."

She hadn't. Much.

Her hazel eyes sparkled and he could see in them that she had meant her words, and she thought his valley was beautiful. It was, and it was probably even more beautiful to someone like her, who had likely come from a city life.

She moved away again, snapped a few photographs and looked at each one. Trying out angles?

He tensed when she moved closer to him, and his gaze tracked her as she passed him, stopping only a metre from him. Her fine dark eyebrows pinched, her shell-pink lips pursing. He was about to ask her what was wrong when she lifted the camera and took another shot. Her eyes lit up when she angled the camera away from her and looked down at it. Happy with the picture?

She crouched again, resting her elbows on her knees, her camera clutched in both hands, ready to lift into place.

He tried to keep still for her, but no matter what he did, he couldn't stop himself from tapping at his leg as he watched her, the energy coursing through him too much to contain.

Another hour passed, and the mist cleared, and he caught the disappointment in her eyes as she gazed at the river, the sparkle that had been in them dying as she rose back onto her feet and lowered her camera. Her shoulders lifted in a long sigh.

"The bears won't be coming today," he said, and she looked at him, the flare of disappointment in her hazel gaze growing brighter as she locked eyes with him.

"Do they really come?" She scanned the river, and the woods on the other side, a look of longing on her pretty face.

Rath nodded. "Sometimes. Something must have spooked them today."

Him.

He was restless around her. The bears were probably picking up on it and steering clear of the creek.

He should have watched her from the cabin instead, keeping his distance so the bears would show up. He wasn't sure why he had come with her, had positioned himself in the open, and hadn't hung back so she could get her photographs.

And go.

A growl curled through him at that thought, his animal instincts rebelling against it in a way that left him cold as something hit him.

His cougar side wanted her.

He wanted her.

It wasn't going to happen. She was human, a complication, and he wasn't looking for a female. He didn't need one in his life.

"Can I stay a little longer?" She fidgeted with her camera, her eyes fixed on it, but they nervously flitted to him when he looked at her. "I drove for days to get here, and then trekked for almost two days, and camped in the woods overnight. I swear, I'll move on in the morning."

Rath frowned at the way she said that, making it sound as if she was talking about doing something other than marching her backside to her vehicle.

"Move on where?" He sat up now, a feeling stirring inside him, one he didn't like.

She looked up river, towards the mountains and the glacier. "This is definitely bear country, and I'm sure I can find some."

He growled inside at that, his cougar side clawing at his skin, pushing for freedom, the thought of her out there in that wilderness, alone and vulnerable, rousing it and instincts long forgotten—a deep need to protect.

He shoved onto his feet, moving so fast she startled and gasped, and loomed over her, so close to her that she had to tip her head back to keep her eyes on his face.

"I thought we'd been through this?" he snapped. "It's dangerous that way. You might end up hurt."

"Attacked?" She swallowed hard and her golden skin paled. "Do you see cougars around here?"

Rath smiled wryly. "All the time."

"Really?" Her hazel eyes widened and darted around, and he swore her cheeks paled further. "I know how to handle bears, but cougars…"

"It's not the cougars who will hurt you." He moved a step closer, just a few inches, but enough that he could feel her heat, drowned in the scent of her, and his damned cougar side stopped frantically clawing at his skull, pushing him to shift and force her to remain. "It's the grizzlies. It's grizzly country up that way."

He was talking shifters, ones liable to attack her on sight, or worse, capture her and keep her.

He looked at Cougar Creek and huffed.

Although, it was a fucking awful time for her to stumble onto his land too.

It wouldn't be long before the males started gathering, and any available female in the vicinity, even a human female, would provoke their instincts to fight for dominance so they could mate with her.

Soon, she would be in as much danger here as she would be if he let her go upstream towards the glacier and the bear shifter pack that called that area of the valley home.

He dropped his eyes to her and stared at her as she looked at her surroundings.

For the first time in three decades, desire stirred in his chest, tore through his muscles and flowed through his veins, and had his cougar side shifting beneath his skin, hungry for a female.

Hungry for her.

Scratch soon.

She had been in dangerous waters from the moment he had set eyes on her.

Her hazel eyes slowly lifted to his, enormous now as she looked at him, but they were dark too, her dilated pupils and her scent revealing the emotions that flowed through her.

Desire. Need.

They called to him, and damn, part of him wanted to answer.

Her eyes darted away from him, and her voice trembled as she spoke. "I... uh... didn't see these cabins on any maps."

"They're all hidden by the trees." Was that his voice, so rough and deep, strained and raw? He tried to tear his eyes away from her, but couldn't, was powerless against her pull as her scent curled around him, her beauty branded itself on him, and her soft curves inflamed him.

A blush climbed her cheeks. "There's a lot of cabins. Do you run a business here? Like vacation rentals?"

Was she thinking of checking in? Fuck, he probably wouldn't turn her away, even when he knew he should.

"They're all family cabins. I just look after them." He mustered the strength to rip his focus from her and pinned it on the cabin nearest the river. The sight of it acted as a bucket of ice down his crotch, instantly cooling him off as he remembered that the family who owned it were coming soon, and so was his brother, and then most of the eligible pride males would hit the creek. "I'm meant to be refurbishing one."

"I'm sorry. I'm getting in your way." She glanced at the cabin and then back at him, and he resisted looking at her, felt her frown and sensed the shift in her emotions, darker ones emerging. His coldness had upset her, and damn, she was quick to bring up a wall around herself and hit him with the same cold front he was showing her. "I'll just get my things and go."

It was for the best.

But he found himself lunging for her, seizing her wrist as his heart froze in his chest, the thought of her leaving propelling him into action before he could think about what he was doing.

She looked down at his hand on her arm.

"You can stay one night." Fuck, he was going to regret this, he knew it, but for some damned reason he couldn't bring himself to let her go just yet. "You can't photograph anything that might give away the location, or me… or any of the cabins. You have to stick to the river and the wildlife, and *do not* wander out of the boundary of the village."

That seemed to scare her, and her eyes leaped to the mountains, her pulse picking up in his ears as she stared at them.

When she finally looked back at him, that pulse kicked faster, echoing in his own chest as she smiled at him, one that reached her stunning eyes.

"Thank you," she murmured, and then added with a frown, "I just realised I never got your name."

"Rath," he uttered, falling under her spell again, feeling a little hazy from head to toe as his cougar side purred at her, had him wanting to rub against her to mark her with his scent.

To make her his.

She tipped her head back, looked deep into his eyes, and rocked his entire world on its axis with three innocent words.

"Thank you, Rath."

CHAPTER 4

Rath couldn't concentrate for shit. He growled as he hit his thumb with the hammer for what must have been the millionth time, lifted the sore digit to his lips and sucked on it as it throbbed. The female responsible for his predicament wandered the riverbank, blissfully unaware of his plight and the damage she had done with three simple words, breathed in a voice that had been far too fucking sultry, had made his name on her lips sound like the sweetest drug, one that had instantly intoxicated him.

One that had made him crave more.

He sank back on his ass and huffed as he set his hammer down beside the pile of shingles and braced his left leg against the roof so he didn't slide down it.

His gaze immediately strayed to the curvy female wreaking havoc on him, a strange sense of calm washing through him the second his eyes landed on her, the restlessness he experienced whenever he focused on his work and not her easing and leaving him at peace.

Gods, she was beautiful.

She moved around his territory as if she belonged there, fitted right in with her practical clothing of natural coloured hiking gear. The browns and beiges suited her, seemed to bring out the hint of a tan in her complexion and the rich chestnut of her hair that tumbled in silky waves from her ponytail.

He studied her as she lifted the camera, moved it around, her finger working the button, and then tilted it away from her and gazed down at the photographs she had taken. Did she know she had a habit of taking four different shots at a time, all of them a slight variation? She would take a landscape one with the lens zoomed out, and then another zoomed in a little, and follow those by tipping the camera to take two similar shots in portrait.

Rath canted his head, warmth curling through his chest that became heat as she removed her dark cream jacket, revealing a fawn-coloured woollen jumper beneath that hugged her breasts and the slight roundness of her belly, and stretched tight over her hips and ass.

Damn.

He dragged his eyes away from her as a need to drop from the roof, prowl over to her and sweep her up into his arms and show her just what she was doing to him slammed into him.

He scrubbed a hand over his mouth and paused with it on his throat as he growled at himself for getting caught up in her. It was just the season. His instincts as a male cougar had been roused, and it was affecting him, making him view her as a female in need.

One he wanted to satisfy.

He shook that desire away and forced his focus back to his work, moving onto his knees on the roof and picking up his hammer again. He reached into the back pocket of his jeans for another nail and positioned the shingle, slipped it into the hole he had drilled in the top left corner, and hammered it into place.

He fell into an easy rhythm, made swift work of a row of fresh shingles, almost managed to forget the human wandering around his territory.

Until she moved closer to him.

His senses sparked again, her proximity making him hyper-aware of her as she walked around behind him, pacing the shore, stopping from time to time to take pictures. He could see her moving around without needing to look at her, could chart her exact position and the fact she was facing away from him, and his hearing sharpened as his focus switched to her, allowing him to hear every click of her camera's shutter.

Every sweet breath she drew.

Every damned sigh she loosed as she admired her work.

And his territory.

She had called it beautiful.

Gods, that made him want to puff his chest out like some damned peacock.

Plenty of people, cougar shifters, had admired his territory. She wasn't the first female to call it beautiful.

But fuck, she was the first one who had affected him with those words.

And the first female in a long time who had affected him by simply saying his name.

It was the season. The damned season. Just because his role during the gathering was that of protector, and overseer in a way, it didn't mean he was immune to its effects. He had needs too, but he didn't need a female in his life.

He didn't want one.

Ivy moved closer still, and he felt her eyes on him as a shiver down his spine, one that spread heat through his veins and stoked his need, birthing a desire to look at her.

He kept his eyes on his work, ignoring her, doing his best to shut her out and pretend she didn't exist.

The sooner she got a damned photograph of a bear and left, the better.

It had been a mistake to let her stay, worse than a mistake to agree to her remaining on his property, close to him, overnight.

He should have made her leave.

He breathed a low sigh of relief when she took her eyes off him and moved away, and he relaxed again, that heat she stirred washing out of him and allowing him to focus back on his work.

Another row of shingles went down quickly, and he was falling back into a nice tempo.

Ivy gasped loudly.

Rath whipped around to face her, a bolt of fear shooting through him, worry that hurled a hundred images of her in danger at him and had him ready to spring off the roof of the cabin and shift to fight whatever had startled her.

To protect her.

He stilled.

She leaped backwards, out of the stream, grimacing as the pebbles on the shore bit into her now-bare feet, and shivered, muttering obscenities to herself beneath her breath.

Her mouth snapped shut and she tensed, and every instinct he possessed said that she had felt him looking at her, was aware a predator watched her, a beast who wanted to fight, seethed with a need to attack.

She slowly turned to look over her left shoulder at him, a pink stain on her cheeks. "It was cold."

That was all she had to say?

She had almost given him a fucking heart attack, had pushed him close to shifting in front of her, a human, revealing his kind to her, and all she could say was it was cold?

He growled at her, "What did you expect? It comes from the glacier."

He pushed out a slow breath, trying to steady his racing heart and purge the adrenaline that had shot through him at the thought she was in danger, and ignored the way she scowled at him. No way he was going to apologise for the bite that had been in his tone.

Who the fuck walked in a glacial river in spring without testing the temperature with their hand first?

He huffed and vaulted from the roof, landing in a silent crouch on the deck, and pushed onto his feet to stride towards her where she stood sheepishly beside the river, her eyes on it now.

Maybe scolding her had been a bit much.

That tight, squirming feeling kicked off in his chest again and he did his damnedest to ignore it as he reached the river, pulled a cloth from his back pocket and crouched beside the crystal clear water. He wetted the handkerchief and rubbed it over his brow and neck, wiping the sweat from it. The water was particularly cold today, more so than normal. The warmer weather was probably melting the snow on the mountains and bringing it down into the river.

He glanced at her feet, at her pinkened toes, and then back at his cloth as he lowered it in front of him.

"You okay?" he said gruffly, sort of an apology, but not an outright one, because he didn't need her getting comfortable around him.

Because he shouldn't be getting comfortable around her.

"Mmhmm." She shuffled along the bank a few inches, away from him, and busied herself with her camera, and that feeling in his chest grew worse, had him wanting to rise onto his feet and apologise to her.

Rath looked down at the water, shoved his damp cloth back into his jeans pocket, and scooped some up, drinking it from his palm. Her eyes landed on him, and he could sense her interest as she watched him, her curiosity as she turned towards him and the spark of anger and irritation he had detected in her faded. He scooped another handful of water up and drank it, sighed as the coolness of it washed through him, chilling that spark of fire in his blood that she kept igniting.

He eased back, pushed his hands against his knees and rose to his full height. "It's clean. Pure. There's nothing but forest and mountains between here and the source."

She still looked wary, and he could understand why, but his cougar senses would warn him if the water was infected with something, and in all his years at Cougar Creek, he had never had a problem drinking directly from the river. Even with his constitution, it was possible for him to become ill if he downed enough bacteria.

"You've never gotten sick from it?" She glanced at the water.

"Never." He kept his eyes locked on her, studying the subtle ways her expression shifted as she considered drinking from the river.

"I've done it once or twice before." Her eyes darted to him and then away again. "I always worry there will be something in it though that will make me ill."

"You won't get sick." When he said that, her hazel gaze leaped to him and she searched his eyes, as if looking for the truth in them, or maybe the reassurance she needed to go through with it.

She must have found it, because she stooped, and his eyes dropped to her as she cupped her hands and scooped water into them, and lifted it to her lips. Her eyes drifted shut as she drank it, and he almost groaned as beads of water chased down her chin and her throat. His cougar side purred in deep appreciation of the sight of her, looking for all the world as if she was made to walk in his one.

She lowered her hands and looked up at him, her gaze catching his and holding it, and as the sun bathed her face, made her eyes sparkle and brightened them, he lost himself in charting every fleck of gold against the hazel of her irises.

His heart beat harder, stronger, drummed against his chest and in his ears as he stared down into her eyes, the air between them crackling with energy that chased over his skin, had the hairs on the back of his neck rising and his breath coming faster.

A need to growl, to snarl and make her cower, make her submit to him, rose within him, had golden fur on the verge of rippling over his arms and chest beneath his dark green fleece.

He shook it and the spell she had cast on him off and pushed away from her, his voice a dark rough rumble. "Only gasp like that when you're about to get attacked in the future."

Because it did things to him that made him dangerous.

Made him want to forget everything.

Made him want to lose himself in her.

CHAPTER 5

"Let me help." Ivy followed Rath as he stormed away from her, his damned back up over her gasping.

It wasn't as if she had committed a crime, so she couldn't understand why he was making such a big deal of it. The iciness of the water had shocked her, and she had done what had come naturally.

Gasped.

Part of her wanted to stay near the river in case bears showed up, and maybe to avoid him a little, but the rest of her had her chasing him down, determined to do something that would stop him from being so gruff with her. Downright moody.

Maybe he was always like this.

Maybe she was expecting too much and any attempt to smooth things over between them so her night here wouldn't be awkward and a complete disaster was going to backfire and only make things worse.

"I don't need help." He proved that by nimbly leaping to land on his right foot on a post of the railing that enclosed the deck that ran around the front and right side of the cabin and vaulting from it onto the roof as if he was a professional gymnast.

"It's the least I can do for you letting me stay here. I want to repay you."

When he glanced down at her, banked heat in his stormy grey eyes, images of other ways of paying him back popped into her head. She immediately shoved them out again.

He turned away and looked as if he was going to ignore her until she got bored and went away, but then he huffed as he glanced around the roof. He stilled and stared at the rafters through the hole he was repairing, his rugged face dark with whatever thoughts were crossing his mind, his near-black eyebrows dropping low, causing a wrinkle at the top of his straight nose and a slight twist of his lips.

He didn't look at her as he spoke. "Fine. Hand me those shingles."

There was a weight of regret in his tone, one that made it clear he wasn't happy about her helping him. Why? Was he the sort of man who preferred to fly solo in everything he did? Did he view her helping as something that would make his work less rewarding?

Or was it something else?

She gathered a stack of the wooden shingles and tiptoed, stretching them towards him as he reached down for them, his eyes fixed on the roof, held away from her.

She was starting to get the impression that his problem wasn't with people, it was with her.

Well, he wasn't the first difficult man she had worked with, and she wasn't going to let his temperament deter her from paying him back by helping him.

While he worked, she took off her camera and set it down on a rusty metal table, and moved the table close to her, so the camera would be within arm's reach if a bear showed up. He had said they wouldn't come today, but what did he know about wild animals? It was impossible to predict their movements. There was still a chance that the bears would show up.

A chance that she clung to as she handed him more shingles whenever he needed them and kept one eye on the river as the day wore on.

"They won't come now," he said and she snapped herself back to him, tearing her gaze away from the river and lifting it to him where he balanced on the edge of the roof, his left leg dangling and his right one bent at the knee.

He rested his arm on it, letting his left one drape with his leg, and looked down at her.

"They might." She tried to keep the disappointed note from her voice, because if she heard it, she would want to give up on them, and she had never given up on anything.

Not yet anyway.

"Something must have spooked them." He raised his head and scanned the scenery beyond her, a wrinkle forming between his dark eyebrows as he set his jaw, focus written in every line of his face. His eyes looked brighter again, almost golden. His deep voice lowered to a smooth warm tone that was soothing. "Maybe they'll show up in the evening."

She glanced at the river and had the feeling he was being nice to her, saying what she wanted to hear so she didn't lose heart, but when she looked at him, his handsome face was dark and he was focused back on his work, hammering in the shingles with a renewed sense of purpose, as if the poor things had done something wrong.

Or maybe he felt he had done something wrong by being nice to her.

It hadn't slipped her notice that he had been keeping his distance. She had known enough men to spot the signs that screamed he wanted her gone, regretted letting her stay and had thought the better of it. It was fine with her. As soon as she got her shots, or tomorrow morning passed without a bear showing up, she was moving on.

She had learned her lesson where men were concerned, was damned if she was going to get caught up in him and get burned all over again.

But damn, he didn't make it easy.

He hammered the last shingle home, admired his work with a satisfied glint in his grey eyes, and then twisted away from the roof. He planted his hands against the edge of it and sprang down, his body flexing deliciously as he pushed off, hips arching forwards, and landed squarely on his feet on the deck just a metre from her.

He must have been a professional gymnast in a previous life.

Although she did suppose his agility could easily have come from working alone on the cabins, his days passed in manual labour and physical exertion making him more flexible and stronger than most men.

He slowly rose to his full height, his eyes darker than before as he lifted them to her, and stared at her for a long, drawn out and intoxicating moment before he casually discarded his hammer and pulled a handful of nails from his back pocket. She tensed as he leaned towards her, heart doing a flip in her chest as he came close to brushing her left arm with his chest, and his masculine earthy scent filled her senses.

The sound of the nails hitting the metal table beside her was loud in the thick silence.

He paused, and she swore he looked at her, swore he leaned towards her a little as he withdrew and pulled in a deep breath.

As if he was taking her scent into his lungs in the way she wanted to breathe his in.

He didn't look at her as he moved around her, but he tensed as his left arm brushed hers.

His voice came from behind her, a note of warmth in it that was new, and a little startling. "You deserve a beer after your work. Come on."

"What I really need is a shower," she muttered as she turned to follow him, sure that she stank after her trek through the forest and today's work.

He paused and looked at the river. "You can wash in it."

Ivy shuddered. "It was freezing. No thank you!"

He smiled, and hell, it was dazzling, lit up his whole face and was such a contrast to the man who had been glowering at her from the moment they had met that all she could do was stare at him and wonder who this man was and when had he switched bodies with the Rath she had thought she had been coming to know?

"I have a bath. The water's heated by the solar panels and the burner, but it should be hot enough. You're welcome to use it." The moment he said that, something crossed his face, something that erased the warmth from him and left her feeling cold as he moved away from her, heading towards his cabin.

Ivy lingered, her gaze following him up the sloping green as his long legs swiftly devoured the distance between him and the cabin as if he couldn't get away from her quickly enough.

Infuriating.

It was definitely a word that applied to him.

He wanted her off his land, and then let her stay. He was nice to her one minute, and biting her head off in the next. He smiled at her, and then hit her with a scowl so fierce she was left reeling.

She wasn't sure she could figure him out if her life depended on it.

As smoke curled from the chimney of his cabin, filtering through the tall pines that sheltered it to blend with the grey of the mountain beyond, she picked up her camera and flicked through the photographs, using them to distract her from him. She didn't need to figure him out.

Tomorrow, she would be gone, and he would be just a memory.

One she was beginning to feel would haunt her for the rest of her life.

She sighed, set the strap of her camera over her shoulder, and trudged up the slope to his cabin. When she reached it, stepping up onto the deck, he emerged so swiftly he almost collided with her.

"You took your time," he grumbled, and she shrugged, because she didn't owe him an explanation. He edged past her as if she had a contagious disease and he didn't want to risk getting it and stepped off the deck. "Bath is filled."

With that, he was striding away from her.

Infuriating man.

She peered into his cabin. It was roomier than she had expected, with a small kitchen area to her right and a rickety looking staircase that curved up to a loft, and a living room ahead of her. She walked to the coffee table and set her camera down beside his laptop, bent and stripped off her boots. She placed them near the log burner and looked around for the bathroom.

A door beyond the couch, opposite the fire, revealed a white tub.

Ivy crossed the room to it and frowned.

Infuriating and complicated.

She canted her head at the neat stack of fluffy white towels folded on the closed seat of the toilet beside the sink near the bathtub, and the arrangement of shampoo and body wash bottles on top of them.

He seemed to hate showing her any kindness, had reacted badly all the times he had been nice to her, and now he had shown a great amount of care, filling the bath for her, presenting her with fresh towels and leaving the cabin so she would have it to herself.

Even if she had all the time in the world, she wasn't sure she would ever figure Rath out.

She leaned back and peered through the kitchen window to her right, but there was no sign of him outside, so she stepped into the bathroom, closed the door behind her, and stripped off, because it felt like months rather than days since she had washed and she didn't want to waste this chance by letting the water get cold.

Not when Rath had obviously used all of his hot water supply to fill the bath as much as he could, to around halfway up the white tub.

She stepped into the tub, sank into the water, and moaned as she leaned back and it lapped over her breasts and shoulders.

Heaven.

Her eyes slipped shut and she relaxed, savouring the way the water warmed every inch of her and seemed to chase the fatigue from her body and the tension from her muscles.

A bath had never felt so luxurious.

She wasn't sure how long she soaked, but the water was growing cooler when she finally forced herself to reach for the shampoo and body wash, and set to work. When she was done, she eased back again, wringing out every last drop of time in the bath.

She didn't want to leave it.

Or put her old clothes back on.

She was sure they stank too and her odour had been half the reason he had been so off with her, keeping his distance. She couldn't blame him.

"Shoot," she muttered as the thought of fresh clothes had her remembering that she had left her pack in the living room, near the door.

Her heart pounded as she considered trying to reach it.

She wasn't sure where Rath was now. She had been in the bath so long that he could be anywhere, had probably gotten bored of waiting for her to emerge and had returned to the cabin for that beer he had clearly wanted as a reward for his hard work.

Ivy stood and let the water run off her, and grabbed one of the towels from the stack. Thankfully, it was large enough to wrap around her, and covered her from her chest to midway down her thighs. She tucked it closed beside her left breast, opened the door and peeked out.

He wasn't in the cabin.

But he had been at some point. The white plastic canisters tucked in the corner of the kitchen were full of water now. Replenishing his supply because of her? She would have to remember to thank him for the bath.

She tiptoed across the room, heart racing as she strained to hear him, afraid that he was on the deck and would hear her and walk in while she was only wearing a towel.

When she reached the wall behind the log burner, and her black backpack that rested against it near the door, she glanced off to her left.

Froze.

Rath stood by the river, his bare back to her, faded jeans riding low on his lean hips. She couldn't take her eyes off him as he twitched a fishing rod back and forth, the line swishing with each swing, his muscles working in a symphony that had her soul singing praises for him. He finally cast, and as soon as the fly settled on the rippling water, he began gently jerking the rod with his right hand, causing the tip to twitch as he slowly pulled on the line with his left, drawing the fly across the river.

Her breath lodged in her throat, and hell, she wanted to grab her camera and take a picture of him because he was stunning, a sight to behold as the sinking sun cast golden light over him and the mountains rose beyond him.

The only thing stopping her was how angry he had been when he had seen she had photographed him.

He struck, leaning back as he lifted the tip of the rod and it bent. It jiggled as he began drawing the line in quicker, the fish fighting back.

When he had it at the bank, he stooped and lifted it, his profile to her, and then his head turned her way.

Ivy dove into the bathroom with her backpack.

She slammed the door shut, and set the bag down, and rifled through the lower section for a fresh set of clothes. Her charcoal trekking trousers were her only spares, and while they were a little tighter than her brown ones, they definitely went better with her chestnut hoody. She loved natural colours, but there was such a thing as too much brown.

She slipped into a fresh set of black underwear, pulled on a merlot-coloured t-shirt, and pushed her arms into her hoody, leaving it open as she shimmied into her trousers.

Her hair came next, a task she never relished. She grimaced as she brushed the tangles from her damp waves and wrestled them back into submission, and debated tying it back. It would dry faster if she left it loose, so she placed her elastic around her wrist and used his toothpaste and her brush to clean her teeth.

When she was done, she eased back and admired her work in the mirror hanging above the sink between the toilet and the bath.

She looked brighter, fresher, and she felt it too.

All the disappointment of not seeing bears today, and the stress of everything that had happened this morning with Rath, drifted away, rose from her shoulders and left them feeling lighter as she smiled at herself in the mirror.

Tomorrow, she would see bears, she was sure of it. She would get her shots.

Ivy pulled the bathroom door open.

Rath lifted his head as he walked into the cabin, and his eyes widened slightly before he looked away, down at his hand as he held up a pair of trout. "I hope you like fish."

He moved into the kitchen, set the fish down on a plate he grabbed from one of the wooden cupboards below the counter, and put them in the small refrigerator. He washed his hands. Thoroughly. Avoiding her again?

She stared at his back, almost disappointed to see he had dressed. The dark green fleece hugged his shoulders, making it easy for her to recall what they had looked like naked, his golden skin stretched tight over mouth-watering muscles. She had sworn off men, but she wouldn't have said no to a closer look at him.

He cleared his throat, the sound a little awkward, and turned towards the refrigerator again as he dried his hands. "Beer?"

She nodded. "Please... and thank you for the bath. It was heavenly."

"No problem." He grabbed two brown bottles, cracked them open and walked out onto the deck without even glancing at her.

Ivy followed him, stopping only to put a pair of socks on, arriving on the deck in time to see him slump into the chair furthest from the door, the one she had occupied this morning, and kick his feet up on the railing of the fence.

His grey eyes locked on the horizon as he lifted the beer to his lips, and her eyes locked on him, drinking in his profile as he tipped his head back slightly. After a few seconds of her staring, he grabbed the other beer he had set down on the low table between the wooden chairs and held it out to her.

Ivy took it and the other seat, wanted to lift her legs as he had but they weren't long enough for her to reach the fence around the deck. She stretched them out in front of her instead and sank into the chair, leaning back with a sigh as she let the beauty of the scenery wash over her again.

The sun was lower now, and it looked as if they were in for a beautiful sunset, perfect for enjoying with a cold beer.

The silence that stretched between them as they sat next to each other, watching the world, was strangely comfortable. Birdsong in the trees brought a smile to her lips, the melody becoming entrancing as it mingled with the sound of his steady breathing and she sipped her beer and waited for the sunset.

"Do you like it out here, in all this wilderness?" She didn't take her eyes off the horizon. The sun was edging past a mountain now, a great jagged peak that had a dusting of snow clinging to it that turned gold in the evening light. "Do you not get lonely?"

She would.

It was beautiful, but it was so quiet.

"I'm a solitary kind of guy." His deep voice rolled over her, warming her as much as the beer. "Everyone who owns a cabin here is like that."

"They don't live here year-round though, and I'm thinking you do." She took another mouthful of beer to stop herself from looking at him as she wanted.

He sighed, the sound more contentment than anger or dissatisfaction. "I like it here and I feel no need to leave."

He was silent for a minute.

And then said something that resonated with her.

"This is home."

CHAPTER 6

Rath wasn't sure why he was telling her anything about himself. It wasn't as if he wanted to know anything about her, or whether it had any point when she would leave tomorrow and he would never see her again.

But as Ivy sat beside him, her eyes on the sunset, swigging her beer, and started idly talking as if she was speaking to herself rather than him, he couldn't help but listen to her.

Found himself aching to know more about her.

"I get that." She smiled at the world. "I feel it too, you know? That connection with nature, that this place is a sort of home to me... like I belong here or something. It's silly."

A part of himself whispered a dangerous question.

What if it wasn't silly, what if the reason he was so aware of her ran deeper than merely the spring affecting him or him finding her attractive?

What if the reason she felt at home here in his territory ran deeper than her simply finding it beautiful, a world away from the cities and their fast pace of life?

Rath didn't want to contemplate the answer to that question, and Ivy mercifully started talking again, filling the silence and his mind with her words, drawing his focus away from the instincts she had awoken in him.

"I hit a slump in my work last year." She scowled at her beer and picked at the label. "I just couldn't get my compositions right. They were lacking something. Or maybe it was me lacking something. I don't know."

She sighed, a deep one that had him looking across at her because it spoke of hurt.

"I was in a bad place for a while." She lifted her head and fixed her eyes on the horizon again. "But I've taken some good shots of the grizzly bears and I'm beginning to feel like my old self again."

He could see the relief as it crossed her face, felt it in her as she tilted her head back and looked at the emerging stars.

She breathed, "God, it's beautiful here. I can see why you like it. You can't really see the stars in the cities."

Rath tipped his head up. They were faint still. She was in for a surprise when the sun sank beyond the horizon and the sky darkened, and part of him was excited to see her reaction, wanted to keep her outside so she wouldn't miss the show nature was going to put on for her tonight.

He had seen it for decades, but it still moved him when he saw the Milky Way stretched above him, a billion stars forming a spine across the night sky.

"My brothers tell me the same thing." He swigged his beer, frowned when the bottle turned out to be empty, and brought his feet down and pushed onto them. He glanced down at her and waggled his bottle. "Another?"

She drained the last of her beer like a pro and smiled as she held it out to him. "Definitely. I was always a beer girl rather than a wine one."

He could see that, and fuck, part of him found it charming that she had a little more country life than big city life in her, looked comfortable in practical clothing and drinking beer, getting muddy and breathing fresh air, rather than fancy dresses and high heels, and posh wine at grand parties.

He took the empty from her and brushed past her, his leg skimming hers. An accident. Definitely an accident.

Although the way she tensed and her pulse leaped had a shiver arcing up his leg and along his nerves, and a need to rub against her rising to the fore again.

That was twice now.

Twice he had brushed her and twice she had tensed, had reacted in a way that screamed she was interested in him.

Gods, he had barely stopped himself from dropping his face to her throat and scenting her when he had been close to her at the river cabin earlier. The need to do it had been fierce, consuming, had driven him to press his nose to her smooth flesh and inhale her, branding her scent on his soul.

Had filled him with an urge to lick her nape.

That had startled him into backing off and pacing away from her before he could even consider why that need had arisen in him.

A need reserved for when a male found his fated one.

The mate who had been made for him.

A true mate.

He froze by the refrigerator and looked out of the window at Ivy.

She couldn't be that for him.

He was just wound up by the season, on edge because of the gathering and her arrival, thrown off balance by her beauty when the urge to mate was strong in him.

A groan tore from his lips as she ran her hands through her thick chestnut waves and stretched, pulling the tangled strands away from her neck, exposing her nape.

Wasn't going to happen.

He shoved his head into the refrigerator to cool off and stared at the gutted fish he had hunted for her, the need to provide for her driving him to the river while she had bathed. Just as it had driven him to run her a bath and gather her enough water in case she wanted another or grew thirsty for something other than beer.

Gods, he wanted her.

He had thought he had built a barrier around his heart during his time at the river, one that would withstand her, but the moment she had emerged from the bathroom, her damp hair down and curling around her shoulders, that damned dark red t-shirt pulled tight over her ample breasts, a sparkle in her hazel eyes and her skin rosy from the heat of the bath, the wall had crumbled.

She was beautiful. Fucking beautiful.

And the fact she now smelled like him in a way, the scent of his bath products all over her, was playing merry hell with him.

He wanted her to smell of him properly, ached with a need to rub his scent all over her and mark her as his.

He growled as he grabbed two more bottles of beer and kicked the refrigerator door shut.

Wasn't going to happen.

He needed her gone tomorrow, before any other cougar shifters arrived. He couldn't have an unmated human female hanging around when fired up males were about to descend on the creek.

Because he would probably end up killing them.

Gods. He set the beers down on the counter and gripped it. The urge to fight would be too strong to resist, the thought of another male trying to claim her pushing him to react, to battle for dominance over her and assert himself as her male.

He needed her gone before anyone arrived.

He snarled at that, his claws lengthening in response to the idea of her leaving him.

Rath stared down at them, shocked by the sight of them, by the ferocity of the need that rocked him to his soul.

He breathed through it, lifted trembling hands from the counter and focused on opening the beers, on a small task that would keep his mind and hands occupied enough that he could shut down his feelings, these urges, and claw back some control.

Because he was dangerous as he was now, liable to do something he might regret.

Like revealing to Ivy that he was no ordinary man.

When the beers were open, and his nails were normal again, he sucked down a hard breath, expelled it and strode out onto the deck.

Ivy glanced up at him. "You took your sweet time."

Gods, she sounded so at ease around him now, so comfortable with him.

He wanted to snap something at her to drive her away, to place more distance between them, but he couldn't bring himself to do it.

"Sorry." He handed her the beer and nursed his own one as he sank into his seat, leaned back and rested his ankles on the railing.

She glanced across at him and smiled. "You were saying something about your brothers?"

Had he been?

He thought back, and realised that he had, and that he had been gone longer than he had thought and had missed the sunset. The sky was growing darker now, the stars brighter.

He watched them as they broke through the fading light above the horizon, beyond the mountains.

"My brothers say the same thing about the cities… about not being able to see the stars. I'll never understand why someone would want to live in such a place." Because the stars were beautiful. Nature was beautiful. It was ever-changing. Even the same scenery could look different every day, altered by the weather, the lighting, or the season.

She shrugged, lifted her beer to her lips, and lowered it again. "Not everyone is made to cope with a life like yours, out here in the wild, not a soul for miles."

Was she?

Rath scrubbed that thought, not wanting to think about it.

"I should set up my tent and bear fence before I get drunk or it gets too dark." Those words leaving her lips left him cold and had him close to growling again.

"No way." He wasn't going to let her sleep out in the open, where she would be vulnerable, not when other cougars were due to return at any moment. He wanted her safe. "You're staying in the cabin with me."

Her eyes widened and leaped to him.

He hadn't meant it like that, but the flicker of heat in her gaze had him considering it.

He pushed out other words than the ones he wanted to say. "You can take my bed and I'll take the couch."

She fidgeted with her beer. "Sure. If you insist."

"Believe me, I insist." Because he was damned if he would leave her unprotected, out here in the dark to fend for herself in some flimsy piece of material, or would allow her to get cold when he had a warm bed she could use.

When she smiled at him, and it hit him hard, had that warmth curling through his veins again, he dragged his eyes away from her and swigged his beer, and reminded himself that she shouldn't be here, couldn't be here. He needed to get her to leave tomorrow, before anyone arrived.

Keeping her around today had been a mistake.

Being near her, around her, was too damn comfortable, and she drew him to her too much. It was only a matter of time before he messed up, before he did something that revealed he wasn't like her and would send her running, exposing his kin to danger and forcing him to move the location of their home again to avoid the hunters.

He stared at the stars and made a vow.

One he was going to keep this time, no matter what.

She was leaving tomorrow.

CHAPTER 7

Rath threw his left arm across his eyes as birdsong roused him from a fitful sleep. It was a miracle he had slept at all. After a few more beers while stargazing and an all too comfortable dinner with Ivy, she had made her excuses and retired up to his bedroom.

It had been hell.

The moment she had left his sight, his senses had locked onto her and tracked her every movement while he had stripped down to his long-sleeved cream t-shirt and black trunks, and arranged himself on the couch. He had done his damnedest to block her out, but it had been impossible.

He could smell her, feel her, and that sensation she stirred in him, the restlessness, had grown stronger.

He had stretched out on the couch, aware of her, that she was close to him, in his bed of all places.

Her breathing had echoed in his ears, the rhythm of it changing as she had fallen into a deep sleep, and gods, it had been difficult to resist the urge to climb the stairs, to look at her while she was sleeping, and stand guard over her, protecting her while she was at her most vulnerable.

It had taken more than an hour to convince himself that she was safe in his cabin, and that he could protect her from his position on the couch, would be aware if anyone entered his home and could easily dispatch them before they could reach her.

Eventually, he had dozed off, into dreams of her that had caused fire to lick through his blood, searing him, making him burn for her.

He bit back a groan, blew out his breath and focused on the loft to check on her, sure she would still be fast asleep.

But the only heartbeat in the cabin was his own.

Rath sprang from the couch, whipping to face the door, his pulse rocketing and senses sharpening, stretching as far and wide as he could reach, hunting for her.

Where was she?

He growled as he grabbed his jeans and yanked them on, his muscles protesting over the sudden surge of action, threatening to cramp as panic seized him in a tight grip, squeezed his heart so hard he feared it might burst.

He was out of the door before he had finished buttoning his fly, scouring the green valley for her. It was barely light, but as he burst from the deck at a dead run, heart pumping hard and senses seeking Ivy, his cougar side shifting relentlessly beneath his skin, sharpening his nails into short claws, the sun broke the horizon, bathing the valley in golden light.

Washing over Ivy where she crouched by the log beneath the tree on the right of the clearing near the river, her camera poised in front of her face, her dark charcoal trousers and deep brown hoody allowing her to blend into her surroundings.

Relief crashed through him, so powerful it almost sent him to his knees.

Gods, he was going to kill her for scaring him like that.

He took a step towards her, and then stilled as he frowned and tracked the aim of her lens.

On the other side of the wide river, just visible through the low mist hanging above the rippling water, a mother black bear emerged from the trees, and two cubs tumbled out behind her, rolling across the stony bank as they played.

A breeze blew, stirring the mist so it danced, swirled and cleared in places, allowing the sunlight to catch on the water, making it sparkle.

The mother bear grunted as she looked back at her cubs, urging them on, and Rath slowly backed off a few steps, aware that she had sensed him. When he was at a distance where his presence wouldn't worry her, he stilled again so he didn't spook them, but kept an eye on them, watching them to make sure the cubs didn't think about crossing the shallow water or notice Ivy.

Protecting her from a distance.

He could shift and reach her before the bear could, would drive it away if he had to, even though it would probably terrify Ivy.

She seemed frightened of cougars.

Rath's gaze drifted to her.

Would she be afraid of him if she saw his other form?

He pushed that question aside as the bear moved on, leading her cubs back into the thick of the forest, and Ivy rose to her feet and checked her camera. She grinned down at the screen and he could feel her excitement, the happiness that flowed through her, despite the distance between them.

When he started towards her, she looked across at him, her smile widening together with her eyes, and gods, as she hurried towards him, a bounce in her step that caused her dark hair to sway in its ponytail, he wanted that excitement she felt, that happiness, to be because it was him she was running to and because she was glad to see him, not because she had managed to photograph the bears.

She was breathless as she stopped beside him, her chest heaving beneath her tight brown hoody, her hazel eyes sparkling as she tilted her head up and they met his.

"Did you see?" She grinned at him, hitting him hard in the chest with it, and he nodded. Her eyes darted back down to the camera, and she checked the photographs again, as if they might have disappeared or been a trick of her imagination. She tilted the camera towards him and moved closer, and he swallowed a groan as she brushed against him, her left arm pressing against his chest. "Look!"

He tried to get his eyes to cooperate, but the way she leaned her head to her right, so he could see the screen of her camera, exposed her throat and he couldn't tear his eyes away from it now that she had tied her hair up again.

Another groan, one that was more of a growl, rumbled up his throat and escaped this time.

She jerked away from him and looked down. "Did I tread on your foot? Why aren't you wearing shoes?"

There was a pretty crinkle to her brow when she looked up at him, as if she thought him crazy to be outside without any boots on.

If he was crazy, it was because he had lost his mind worrying about her.

Ivy flashed the camera his way again, her thumb pressing on the button that made it scroll through the shots she had taken.

"They're good," he murmured, and cleared his throat because it had come out too damned huskily.

A hint of a blush climbed her cheeks and she looked up at him again, her eyes bright and smile infectious.

Godsdamnit she was beautiful.

It hit him hard in the gut, and in the chest, a one-two punch that robbed him of his breath and had him staring down at her in silence, a little dazed and lost in her.

So lost that he didn't pay attention to what she was saying as she spoke to him, her coral-pink lips moving in enticing ways, filling his head with thoughts of silencing her with a kiss. When she looked as if she expected an answer, and he didn't have a clue what she had said, he panicked.

"Yes." There was a fifty percent chance she had asked a question, and a chance that answer was the right one.

Her face lit up. "Oh, thank you! Honestly, I'm not sure why I was so worried... but when I saw the bear and her cubs, I just knew I had to stay and try to get more pictures of them. Did you see them playing? They were adorable. Rolling around like that."

Hang on.

A cold sensation washed through him as he caught up.

A sinking one followed it when she continued speaking at a million miles per hour.

"I shouldn't have worried, but you're not exactly the easiest person to deal with... it's such a relief you said yes. I'll be out of your hair tomorrow. I swear."

Wait, he wasn't the easiest person to deal with?

He frowned at her for that one. He wanted to see how she would have behaved if she had been in his shoes, if he had been the one to come crashing into her territory, and her life, when she already had enough problems to deal with, and triggered a need in her that showed no sign of going away, was only getting stronger the more time she spent with him.

"You don't look so sure now." Her smile faded and she lowered her camera.

He caught the flare of disappointment in her hazel eyes.

But it wasn't the thought of upsetting her that had him shrugging it off and saying, "Not at all. Another night is fine."

It was the thought of her walking and camping overnight to reach her car.

It was the thought that she might meet a cougar on the path when she was alone.

Gods, that disturbed him, had him on the verge of growling.

He needed to stay here tonight and wait for his brother to arrive tomorrow. As soon as he showed up, Rath could walk her back to her car and ensure she made it there safely.

He stared down at her as she checked her pictures again, her smile dazzling, her eyes shining with the happiness he could feel in her.

"Breakfast first, and then you're on helper duty again." He drank in the smile she turned on him, the way she looked at him as if nothing would make her happier than spending the day with him again, working with him, and wanted more.

Grew greedy with a need to have all her smiles to himself.

A gentle breeze swept around her, blowing strands of her hair across her cheek as she looked back down at her camera, her eyes on the screen again.

Rath absently lifted his hand and reached out to her, and paused on the verge of brushing those rogue strands of chestnut back behind her ear.

He lowered his hand to his side before she noticed and steeled himself, piecing together a wall around his heart that he knew wouldn't protect him, or stop the pain that beat inside him as he thought about tomorrow.

He would escort her to her car, protecting her from his kin and the wildlife.

He just wasn't sure he would be able to convince himself to let her go when he got her there.

CHAPTER 8

Ivy was about ready for another hot bath. She swiped the back of her hand across her forehead and sat back on her heels to admire her work on the deck of the riverside cabin. Rath came out of the door behind her, his boots appearing in view to her left as he stopped beside her.

She tilted her head back and looked up at him.

His steel grey eyes darted over her work as he wiped his hands on a dirty cloth, the muscles in his forearms rippling beneath his golden skin. He had ditched his fleece at some point and had pulled up the sleeves of his black long-sleeved t-shirt that hugged his figure, revealing everything to her.

Damn guy had the body of a god hidden beneath that garment.

His gaze drifted to her. "Good work."

It was?

She looked at the planks she had drilled into place and pursed her lips. It did look good to her. She had never picked up a power tool or done anything remotely DIY in her life, but it wasn't as hard as it had always looked.

Although, she was going to leave the roofing to Rath, and repairing stoves definitely fell under his jurisdiction too.

He pushed the dirty cloth into the front right pocket of his dark jeans, tugging her focus down to his strong hands and legs that went on forever.

"Is it beer o'clock?" Ivy gripped the railing to her right and pushed onto her feet before he caught her staring, stooped and picked up the drill and set it down in the case on the small metal table.

She snapped it shut and looked at Rath.

His eyes zipped from her backside up to her face, and she swore there was a little more gold in them.

Maybe she wasn't the only one with a staring problem.

A flush of heat swept over her skin at the thought he had been looking at her, stoking the fire she had fought a few times over the past day and bringing it back to inferno level. Apparently, the sight of Rath hard at work doing manual labour was a major turn on and one she hadn't been able to deny, no matter how many times she had reminded herself she had sworn off men.

There had just been something alluring and magnetic about him as he had worked on the roof, hammer in one hand and nails held between his flattened lips, his handsome face fixed in a frown as he had focused on the repairs, oblivious to her staring. His muscles had rippled and danced so beautifully with every blow of the hammer, every flex of his body as he reached for another shingle and positioned it, and she had been caught up in him whenever she had taken a break.

He hadn't helped matters when he had shown her how to use the drill to fix the planks to the deck, his body crowding hers as he instructed her on the correct way to hold it and how to change the bits so she could go from drilling to screwing. She had burned fiercely from the feel of his front against her side, his arms encircling her and making her deeply aware of how big he was, how strong his body was beneath his clothing, and how good he smelled.

She had been a wreck for the first few planks he had handed to her after he had cut them to size, and had only managed to recover after he had headed inside to continue work on the stove, leaving her alone to deal with the deck.

When he looked off to his right, towards the river, she did too, and her eyes widened when she saw the sun was almost below the horizon. She hadn't noticed it was getting that late, had been convinced it was early afternoon still.

She picked up her camera from the table, switched it on, and flicked through the images to find the ones she had taken of the male black bear that had wandered through the area while she had been working on the cabin with Rath.

Her eyebrows rose at the time on the screen. Hell, she had thought the bear had visited before noon, but it had been closer to three.

She smiled at the photographs, a satisfied hum buzzing in her veins at the shots she had gotten of the male bear, capturing him drinking at the river and then chasing something in the water.

She couldn't wait for tomorrow and the chance the mother bear might bring her cubs back. She had asked Rath more times than she could count about whether he thought they would, and every time he had half-smiled and said he was sure of it, that it wasn't the first time he had seen them pass along the river in the morning.

Rath moved past her, stealing her attention, pulling it to him as he tidied up the deck, tossing tools back into a grey holdall that had seen better days. One of the screwdrivers he placed in the bag poked out of a rip in the side, and he scowled at it, his dark eyebrows dipping low as he prodded the tip to push it back inside.

When he was done, she slung the strap of her camera around her neck and picked up the drill case.

"Beer time." The way his eyes lit up said he was looking forward to opening a cold one and kicking back on the deck to enjoy what was left of the sunset.

She glanced at it and decided she was going to follow suit. She would have that bath she badly wanted after she had savoured the beauty of the sunset and had seen the stars emerge.

When she looked back at Rath, he was staring across the clearing, his handsome face etched in dark lines and his eyebrows knitted hard above his grey-gold eyes.

Ivy followed his gaze and frowned as her eyes landed on a beautiful raven-haired woman in her twenties walking towards them, an older woman who had to be her mother beside her. While the older woman wore dark green hiking trousers and a thick black jacket, the younger woman wore tight blue jeans that hugged her thighs and the swell of her hips, and a sapphire jumper that accentuated her curvy waist and breasts. Her obsidian waves bounced around her shoulders with each confident step and brushed her rounded cheeks, and she lifted her hand and delicately swept them from her face, revealing dark pink lips and bright grey eyes.

Ivy looked back at Rath, and the way he continued to stare at the woman roused something inside her.

Something she didn't like.

She looked down at herself, at her charcoal trousers and her merlot t-shirt that revealed curves far more sumptuous than the ones on the black-haired woman. Who was she kidding? Of course Rath would look at the younger, more beautiful woman like he wanted her.

Hadn't *he* done the same thing to her?

Traded up.

"I have to deal with this." Rath's deep voice didn't warm her as it swept over her this time.

It left her cold.

She didn't look at him, just stepped off the deck and started walking, because she wasn't sure she could bear seeing him looking at the beauty with eyes dark with desire, and she certainly wasn't going to stick around to hear what they had to say to each other.

She kept her head down as she passed the two women.

"Rath," the older woman said, a note of warmth in her tone, but also a hint of something akin to a demand. "Have you considered our proposition? Ember would like to know whether she can expect you to take care of her."

Heat burned Ivy's heart, and she slowed her step, her blood on fire and breath lodged in her throat as those words registered, the meaning behind them clear, and she waited to hear his response.

"It's good to see you again. Your cabin is ready." Not a denial. Not a yes, either, but it wasn't a denial.

And that stung.

Ivy doubled her pace, hurrying away from him now, not wanting to hear anything else, because she couldn't take it. She had been an idiot. Again. She had stupidly let herself get caught up in her time here, had let herself get caught up in Rath, had sunk into this world and been swept up in it.

It was all make-believe.

She didn't belong here, and tomorrow she would be gone, and she would never see Rath again.

Tomorrow couldn't come quickly enough.

She dumped the drill on the deck of his cabin, bent and wrestled with her laces on her boots, a frustrated growl slipping from her lips when they refused to cooperate. She huffed and her face screwed up as she kicked at them, shoving them off her feet, and left them scattered on the deck, not giving a damn.

She stormed into his cabin, grabbed her backpack and sank onto the couch. She opened his laptop, switched it on, and pulled the memory card from her camera while she waited for it to boot up. Thankfully, her adapter was in the zipped compartment on the underside of the lid of her bag, so she didn't have to tear her entire pack apart to find it.

Her fingers shook as she shoved the memory card into the device, and then put it into the USB port on his laptop. She brought up a browser, and opened her email, sifted through a few of them but found nothing interesting. She started a new email and typed in a name.

Alexander Lord.

The bastard.

Tears threatened to fill her eyes but she dashed them away, refused to let everything get to her. She was stronger than this.

She flexed her fingers and stared at the screen, heart pounding as she considered what she was doing. She hated him, but he had money, far too much of it, and she needed some if she was going to move on.

She hammered out a quick message to him, dispensed with the formalities and got straight to the point, telling him that she had shots of black bears and wanted to go in search of spirit bears next, but staying at their location would be expensive and she would need to work with a guide or two who knew the bears and the area.

She attached a few of her photographs of the black bears, sure they would convince him to send funds to her bank account. He had been supporting her for a few years now, funding her trips to photograph wildlife. She wasn't the only one he supported.

Around a year ago, she had met the other wildlife photographers he funded at a grand gala.

And had made the biggest mistake of her life.

It was all the champagne's fault.

And Alexander's too.

She clicked send and refused to regret asking him for money when he had been a bastard to her. He owed her.

He owed her for screwing her, leaving her in the dead of night and then acting as if nothing had happened when she had contacted him.

She leaned over, rested her elbows on her knees and clutched her head, pushing her fingers through her dark hair.

That ache in her chest grew fiercer, stealing her breath, and she sniffed, held back the tears and tried to purge the pain, tried to let it go even when she knew it wouldn't, not while her head was full of Rath with that woman.

One her mother wanted him to be involved with.

"There you are." Rath's tone lost all warmth as he stopped in the doorway. "What are you up to?"

She scrubbed her eyes, her actions small so he wouldn't notice, and looked at his laptop. "Emailing a few shots to one of my sponsors. I need money so I can move location."

He moved into the room, and cold swept over her as he grabbed his computer and she caught the darkness in his eyes, the twist to his expression that said he wasn't happy about that.

Her emailing her sponsor some pictures, or her leaving?

She stood and tried to take the laptop from him. "You can't snoop in my emails."

He turned a thunderous glare on her. "I can when you're emailing people photographs of my land."

That glare only darkened as he returned it to the screen and clicked, clicked, and clicked.

His irises turned stormy grey, the corners of his mouth twisting downwards as his jaw tensed and his eyebrows dipped low.

"I said no pictures of the cabins. I said just the river and the bears." He spun the laptop to face her and barked, "You want to explain this to me?"

Ivy tensed, her heart lodging in her throat, hammering there as she stared at the screen, at the image of the river and the mother bear with her cubs, and realised that in the corner of it, one of the cabins was visible.

"I didn't... I wouldn't... I didn't notice." She lifted her eyes to his, but the darkness in them left her cold, the rigid line of his jaw telling her that her excuses weren't going to fly.

She backed off a step, her pulse pounding faster as his eyes turned more gold than grey, and her fight or flight instinct kicked in.

Telling her to run.

The savage twist to his expression as he closed in on her didn't help, only made her want to bolt.

"What do you know about this guy you sent the photographs to?" he snapped and towered over her, a wall of muscle that exuded the rage she could see in his eyes and hear in his voice. "You sent him pictures without my permission... pictures that show a cabin and the peaks... those fucking peaks can easily be used to identify this location!"

Ivy flinched and leaned back, curled into herself as she tilted her head away from him, tears lining her lashes as she closed her eyes.

Her voice came out small and weak, uncertain. "He's just my sponsor. He funds my work, and other wildlife photographers too."

"That's not telling me what I want to hear, Ivy. I want to know who the fuck he is and I want to know now. Is he a hunter?"

"No!" She whipped her head up and glared at him. "He's just a man with too much money and he gets tax breaks by funding us. That's all. He has galleries where he displays our works, runs benefits and fundraisers using them to show endangered species in need of help."

"Sounds like a fucking saint." He waggled the laptop at her, his face only darkening. "But even saints can have another agenda, Ivy. How well do you really know him?"

Not as well as she had thought, that was for sure, but she wasn't going to tell Rath that.

"You're being unreasonable." She shoved past him, heading for the door, her temper at boiling point as she remembered how he had treated her when she had arrived on his land, a reminder she had badly needed to clear her head and her heart of any misplaced feelings for him. "Not everyone is a hunter, Rath... but then I don't think you'll ever understand that. You think everyone is out to get you... or at least almost everyone. I guess some people are welcome here."

"Where are you going?" he growled. "We're not done here."

"We're done." She lashed the words at him with all the anger, all the hurt she held inside her, but refused to turn on him like she wanted, because she wasn't strong enough to look at him right now, not without wavering.

She had made her decision.

Tomorrow, she was leaving, and she would never see him again.

She stepped out into the rising darkness before he could say another word, shoved her feet into her boots and didn't bother with the laces as she hit the grass, striding down it towards the river, her blood on fire and her heart thundering as anger swirled with hurt, mixed with bitter disappointment and a hell of a lot of self-reproach.

Ivy swiped at her tears, cursing them as they fell, cursing herself with them.

Fuck, she had been such an idiot again, getting swept up in someone.

She blew out her breath and sucked down another as she wrestled with her out of control feelings.

Part of her screamed to leave now, to grab her camera and backpack and just start walking away from Rath, but she shut out the tempting words, listening to the voice of reason instead.

The one that said heading out in the darkness while her head and her emotions were all over the place was a sure-fire way of running straight into trouble.

She slammed into something near the river.

Something warm and muscular, and big.

She tipped her head up as she stepped back.

Moonlight turned the immense man's eyes silver as he stared down at her and threaded his softly spiked sandy hair with white highlights.

"Sorry." She scrubbed the heel of her right hand across her cheeks and went to step around him.

"What are you doing here?" He caught her arm, his grip gentle.

His voice wasn't. It had a hard note that made her think of Rath, and how he had questioned her when she had first arrived on his property.

More tears came.

Hell, she hated them.

Hated feeling weak and stupid.

"I just needed some air." She rubbed the new tears away, sucked down a breath and exhaled hard, struggling to centre herself and stop more from coming.

She was done with them. No more tears.

No more crying over men who didn't deserve her.

"Air?" The man cocked his head to his left and regarded her with a curious look as he released her arm and adjusted his pack on his shoulder.

Another visitor?

He looked a little like Rath, but he was bigger, not in height but in build, packed with muscle beneath his dark jacket and jeans. He was a good few years younger than Rath too, looking more like early thirties than late.

She nodded.

"Why are you here anyway?" He had asked that question before, and she realised now he hadn't meant why was she storming hellbent towards the river, balling her eyes out like some heartbroken girl?

He wanted to know why she was in the area, on Rath's land.

He looked and sounded too much like Rath to be anything other than one of his brothers, and clearly the obsession about this parcel of land ran deep in all of them, had them struggling to trust anyone they found on it that they didn't know.

"Are you going to start accusing me of being a hunter too? Because I've been through that with Rath," she snapped and frowned at him, her anger rising again, drying up her foolish tears. "I'm here photographing the bears."

She tried to leave it at that, but everything surged inside her, and she couldn't stop her mouth from motoring along without her consent as it all crashed over her again.

"I was feeling good about myself for the first time in a while too… my photos are great… and it's so peaceful and relaxing here, and then he ends up shouting at me and I'm not even sure what I did wrong."

She was ranting, but the man didn't seem to care, just kept his steady gaze on her, his handsome face placid and unreadable.

"Rath?" he said, and she nodded, and a flicker of a frown danced on his brow.

"He let me photograph the bears after I explained to him that I wasn't a hunter."

The man went to touch her shoulder.

Rath's hand clamped down on his wrist and pulled his arm away from her before he could make contact, his voice as hard as diamonds and his expression matching it as he looked at the man. "It's late, and you need to go check on your cabin."

The man looked at him and a slow smile teased his lips as he dropped his gaze to her. "Don't let him boss you around."

With that, he was gone, walking away. She turned and watched him go, tracking him as he crossed the grass, heading towards the far corner of the clearing, near Rath's cabin.

When she looked at Rath, he was scowling at the man's back.

He lowered dark eyes to her. "You need to go back to the cabin."

"No." She stood her ground when he glared at her. "I'm not going anywhere until you explain what's going on here… why you shouted at me."

He huffed, scrubbed a hand over his dark hair and looked around at the clearing. "This place… it's meant to be a secret. It's sacred… a sanctuary that my family is responsible for protecting. The photographs you sent... Ivy, someone could use them to identify the area."

Did he want to protect the bears or the people who owned cabins here?

The thought of him wanting to protect the people seemed ridiculous, so she settled on it being the bears. He had been adamant about hunters, had been convinced she had been one until he had seen her photographs. She could understand his passion for protecting the wildlife from people who illegally hunted it.

"Do you get a lot of hunters?" she said, and when his face darkened, she wanted to sigh, because she felt sure they were going to end up arguing again, and she was tired of it, just wanted things to be as they had been earlier today, when he had smiled at her and been nice. "I know they're a problem in some parts, and I can see why they might be a problem here too. It's nice you want to keep the animals safe, and I'm sorry I sent the pictures without showing them to you first."

His face softened, some of the darkness lifting from it, and he sighed and looked off to his right, to the river and the mountains.

"Ivy," he murmured, his voice like honey, smooth and rich in her ears, and his gaze swung down to her. "I need to know about this man... I need to know everything."

She nodded.

She would tell him what she knew about Alexander, so he could see that he wasn't a threat to this place and so they could move past what had happened tonight.

But she was damned if she was going to tell him everything.

CHAPTER 9

Rath didn't want to know about this male Ivy had sent the photographs to, one who had been quick to respond to her email with a promise that she could have the funding she needed to go in search of spirit bears, but he needed to know, even when he was sure her answers were only going to anger him.

Not because the male was a danger to his kin, and this place, but because he meant something to her.

"I met Alexander maybe three or four years ago now, at a benefit." She turned her profile to him and looked at the river, and the moon as it rose full and beautiful, casting pale light over her skin and turning it milky, and her eyes almost blue. "One of my other sponsors introduced us. I can tell you about him too if you want?"

She glanced at him.

He shook his head. "I'm only interested in the one you sent the pictures to."

The one he felt sure he needed to kill.

"He funded me on a trip to photograph snow leopards in the Himalayas, because a few of my sponsors couldn't afford the expense that year. We kept in touch as best as we could given the remoteness of the area I was trekking through to find them, and when I returned, he was so pleased with the photographs I had managed to get that he invited me to display them at a gala he was hosting to raise funds for protecting them." She sighed, a hint of a smile on her lips that he didn't like, because it stemmed from this male, from something he had done for her, complimenting her and her work, and giving her the means to do what she was passionate about. "The benefit was a big success, and he asked me to do a series on tigers next, because many of the species are on the brink of extinction."

"Sounds like a real hero," Rath drawled and weathered her glare.

She regarded him with eyes that gave none of her feelings away, were devoid of emotion and almost cold. "He's just doing what he can to protect the big cat species."

He suspected otherwise, but kept that to himself, because he was tired of her being angry with him. When she had shouted at him, lashed out with words that had cut deep because they had been heavy with truth, and had stormed out into the night, his first urge had been to chase after her.

He had ended up licking his wounds instead, giving her time and space that she needed.

The email had come in from the male, and he had read it, and checked the photographs again, hoping that the bastard wouldn't be able to identify the location from them.

He had closed his computer and forced himself to relax, to let all his anger bleed out of him.

The moment it had dropped from a raging boil to a simmer, he had sensed his brother, and had stepped out onto the deck to look for him.

The sight of him close to touching Ivy had hit him hard, and he had exploded from the deck, had crossed the distance between them with all the speed he could muster.

Damned if another male was going to touch *his* female.

His brother was lucky he had tamped down the need to fight him.

He had caught the look in Storm's eyes as he had told him to go to his cabin though, the one that had questioned him at the same time as it had revealed he knew the female was something to him, had him rattled and on edge, wanting to fight for her.

"Look, Alexander is just a man who likes to do what he can to help wildlife." Her soft words did nothing to soothe him.

They had the opposite effect, stoking the anger he had managed to leash.

"Your email was curt, not the sort of way you would speak to someone you like and admire, someone who has been kind to you."

She averted her gaze.

"He did something to upset you." Rath knew it, because he was in the same boat, on the receiving end of the same cold and business-like manner because he had upset her.

"It's not really any of your business."

Those words hit him hard, had a growl curling up his throat as that restless feeling returned, urged him to make her see that it was his business, because he could read between the lines.

Something had happened between her and this son of a bitch.

He reached for her arm, determined to take her back to the cabin, to continue their conversation there and uncover just what had happened between her and the male she had emailed.

"Rath?" Ember's gentle voice came from the darkness and Ivy tensed, her shoulders going rigid and her eyes darting away from him, lowering to the grass. "I need to speak with you a moment."

Not now.

He had more pressing matters that needed his attention.

That pressing matter strode away from him, heading back towards his cabin so quickly it was as if her ass was on fire.

Godsdamnit.

"What is it, Ember?" he bit out, and she flinched away from him. "I don't have time for this. I told you I'm not interested. Find another male."

She glanced over her shoulder at her cabin. "Mother wants it to be you."

She didn't though. He could see that. She wasn't interested in him as a mate, or even as a male. Her mother had always made it sound as if she was, but now he could see her mother was as meddling as his parents had been. They had picked his mate for him, and while he had come to love her in the short time they had been together, part of him had always wondered if he would have picked her for himself.

Or whether another female would have been the one to win his heart.

He looked off to his left, towards Ivy as she disappeared into his cabin. "I'm sorry, Ember. It's a no."

He turned away from her, damn near sprinted back to his cabin, determined to do something about Ivy. He just wasn't sure what.

When he reached the door, all he could do was stare.

Ivy moved around the living room, shoving things into her backpack.

"What are you doing?" His words sounded distant, as hollow as he felt inside.

She unscrewed the lens on her camera, placed a cap over the hole in the body and on the bottom of the lens, and packed them away. "I'll leave at first light."

The ice in her tone sent a chill down his spine.

She didn't look at him. She kept her eyes on her work, every item she placed in her pack tearing another piece of strength from him, pushing him closer to the edge as a need to make her stay ignited inside him.

"Why are you so eager to leave now?" he bit out as he stepped into the room, that hollow feeling growing stronger every second, making him feel as if everything was draining out of him. All the light. All the warmth. It was all leaving with her. "You want to photograph the bears in the morning."

She didn't answer him, just shoved her brown trousers into the bottom of her backpack with such ferocity that he wanted to cross the room and make her stop, wanted to hold her and make her talk to him, tell him why she was doing this.

She couldn't leave.

Not yet.

He needed more time with her.

"The bears will come, and you'll miss them." It was a poor attempt to make her stay a little longer, just a few hours more, as much time as he could get with her before she needed to go for her own safety.

He felt like a bastard when she paused at her work for a heartbeat and tears spilled onto her cheeks, her hurt going through him.

He hadn't meant to wound her, or maybe he had. Maybe he had used the one thing he could to make her remain with him, her love of the bears, the excitement she had been buzzing with all day because she had been looking forward to tomorrow morning and seeing them again.

She pushed away, taking her black bag with her, turning her back on him.

"I'll go with you. My brother is here now to take care of—"

"No," she snapped and her shoulders shook, her voice wobbling. "It's best I go alone. Maybe I should just go now."

Like hell that was going to happen.

"Why are you so hellbent on leaving now?" He slammed the door of the cabin shut behind him and stormed over to her, grabbed her arm and spun her to face him.

Her bloodshot hazel eyes lifted to his for a second and then she turned her face away from him, lowering it so he couldn't see them.

Too late. They had already done their damage, had driven a spear through his heart and left him cold.

His voice dropped to a strained whisper as he struggled to figure out what he had done wrong, and what he could do to make her stay. "Is this because I was angry with you?"

She shook her head, sending more tears cascading down her reddened cheeks. "No."

"Why then, Ivy?" He lifted his hands, framed her face and brought her head around. She refused to look at him, stared at his chest, and he sighed as he brushed the pads of his thumbs across her cheeks, wiping her tears away. "Tell me what I did wrong... because I don't understand... and I need to understand."

Because he needed to take her pain away. It was vital, like breathing. His female was hurting, and he was sure he was the cause of it, but nothing he did soothed her, and he couldn't make her feel better until he knew the source of her pain.

She jerked out of his grip and rounded the couch, heading for the stairs to the loft.

No, she wasn't going to run away from him. He wouldn't let her. Couldn't.

He blocked her path before she reached them and she glared up at him.

"Don't you need to speak with Ember about something?" she barked and her anger hit him hard, knocked him back a step as he stared down into her fierce hazel eyes. "I just want to sleep now. Please get out of my way."

Like fuck that was going to happen, not now that he had picked up one vital emotion in her.

Jealousy.

"What did you hear?" He moved right and left when she tried to get past him, blocking her attempts.

She huffed and slammed a hand into his chest, tried to shove him but didn't move him at all as he braced himself. "I heard enough. You're meant to be with her, or something."

That 'or something' had a weight of doubt hanging around it.

"She's very beautiful. I'm sure you'll be happy with her."

"Maybe I would be." Not the right words to say, he got that message loud and clear as she gasped and looked up at him, her anger and pain flaring in her eyes, and on his senses. "What's it to you anyway? You're clearly sleeping with your sponsor."

Her eyes widened and she spluttered, "It was one time, a year ago, and it was a mistake. The biggest fucking mistake of my life."

Well, at least he hadn't stolen that title just yet.

She shoved away from him, dumped her bag on the couch and whispered, "He wasn't interested in me like that... I was just another conquest."

A shiver went through him and it brought fire in its wake. Son of a fucking bitch. She had said she had hit a slump last year, had lost her passion for her work, and it couldn't be coincidence that she had slept with the man around that long ago, and was calling it a mistake now. The bastard was responsible for it, had hurt her and made her lose faith in her work and in herself.

She wrapped her arms around herself, her voice small.

"I guess I wasn't pretty enough... or thin enough..."

Rath growled as anger surged through him, her pain stoking it, her belief that she wasn't good enough for the fucking asshole who had hurt her, and she fell silent.

He took a hard step towards her.

She was more than pretty. She was beautiful.

Another step.

She was curvy, and sensual, and fucking perfect in his eyes.

Another one.

He pressed against her back, brought his hands down on her shoulders and pretended they weren't trembling as he skimmed them down her arms, as his heart laboured and a need to prove to her just how perfect she was, just how beautiful he thought she was, ran through him.

He caught her arms and spun her to face him.

Swallowed her gasp in a bruising kiss.

CHAPTER 10

Ivy pushed against Rath's broad chest before she could get swept up in his kiss and the sensations detonating inside her, need that instantly flared hot in her veins and had her aching to go along with things.

She couldn't, not when it would only hurt her in the end.

"You don't have to do this." She pressed her palms to his pectorals as he tried to kiss her again.

"Do what?" There was a confused tilt to his eyebrows as he drew back and looked down at her.

"Pity me." She couldn't look at him as she said that.

He lowered his hands to her hips and stroked his thumbs up and down her sides. "Pity? Believe me, Ivy, the last thing I'm feeling here is pity."

She wanted to believe that, but given the circumstances, and what she had said before he had pulled her into his arms for a kiss that had been too damn delicious, she found it hard.

He dropped his lips to her throat, maddening her with light sweeps of them across her flesh, and husked, "I'm done fighting this feeling... this need. I wanted you the second I set eyes on you, Ivy, and that's the truth."

It was?

Damn, she wasn't sure why she found that so hard to believe when she felt the same way, had been aching for him from the moment he had walked out of that mist.

When his lips found hers again, she didn't stop him. She wrapped her arms around his neck and kissed him back, matched his fervour as he pulled her against him and deepened the kiss, swept his tongue over hers and moaned into her mouth. It pulled a moan from her chest too, had her clinging to him as she kissed him, swept up in the need that had been building inside her for two days now, desire that had her spinning out of control.

He made a low growling noise in his throat, one that was more animal than man, had a thrill chasing through her as he grabbed her backside and lifted her, and carried her to the wall. She moaned as he pinned her against it, looped her legs around his waist and couldn't stop herself from rocking against him, her breaths coming faster as she kissed him, each one choppy and wild.

Fierce.

He pressed his hips forwards, tearing a groan from her as she felt his hardness, and tore another from her as he broke the kiss and pulled his t-shirt off, revealing glorious rope after rope of muscle.

Before she could get her fill of touching him, he had his hands on the hem of her own t-shirt and was lifting it, forcing her arms above her head. A flare of self-consciousness burst inside her, and she wanted to cover herself as he tossed her t-shirt aside and gazed at her, but the way he groaned, the hunger that lit his eyes, need breaking through in their stony grey depths, had her letting him get a good look at her curves.

"Fuck, you're beautiful, Ivy," he breathed and swooped on her lips again, sending heat flashing through her.

She arched against him, moaned as she kissed him and his body pressed against hers, silk over steel, all hard to her softness. He gripped her backside and kissed her harder, his desperation matching hers, and she felt as if everything had been building to this, to a crescendo that stole all control from her and made her a slave to sensation, to the needs pouring through her.

Ivy plastered her hands against his chest, groaned and trembled as his muscles flexed beneath her palms, his strength beneath her fingertips, stirring a deep primal need in her, one that had her desperation mounting. She needed him, and she needed him now, wanted him inside her, was sure she might die if it didn't happen soon.

He groaned as she drifted her hands down his chest, over every delicious peak and valley of his abs, her pulse pounding faster, nerves threatening to rise as she inched her caress lower, moving closer to the waist of his jeans.

"Ivy," he husked, a plea in his deep voice that was her undoing.

All control shattered and all that mattered was touching him, feeling him.

Having him.

She wrestled with the buttons of his jeans, her breaths matching his as they came faster, and he lowered his head to her throat, each sweep of his lips and his tongue sending shivers down her spine, cranking her belly tighter.

She moaned in time with him as she twisted her hand towards him and slipped it into his trunks, skimmed her palm down the rigid hot length of him. He paused against her throat, big body shaking against her as she stroked him, thumbed the tip and smeared the bead of moisture into it.

His breath was hot on her throat, coming in sharp bursts as he remained frozen against her, hemming her in against the wall, his hands shaking against her backside as he held her aloft.

She swore she could feel his need, that it ran through her too, urged her to free his cock so she could stroke it properly, could feel every inch of him.

She released him and pushed at his jeans, shoving them down to his thighs, and he growled and kissed her throat again as she moved towards him. She circled his length with her hand, managed a few strokes that elicited grunts from him before he drew back and dropped her to her feet.

She didn't stop him as he tackled her dark grey trousers, unbuttoning them and pushing them down her legs. He groaned as he revealed them, looking like a man starved as he gazed down at them through hooded eyes that looked more gold again.

Ivy toed her boots off and helped him, desperately kicked off her trousers and didn't give a damn where they landed. She reached for her black panties but he beat her to it, slipped his fingers into them and teased her with a brush of their tips across her mound, ripping a moan from her and sending a thousand volts shooting through her entire body. She sank against the wall, a little breathless as he pushed her underwear down her legs, too slow for her liking, torturing her.

When he reached her ankles, she lifted each foot in turn, helping him because she wanted him back against her, needed his flesh on hers, his lips on hers, was going to go insane if he didn't come back to her soon.

He groaned as he dipped his head and kissed up her thigh, his breath teasing her skin, cranking that need even tighter. She couldn't do slow, wasn't sure how he could, not when this need had been building inside her for what felt like an eternity now.

She threaded her fingers in his thick hair, gripped it and earned a growling sound from him, and pulled him up to her. He caught her legs as he rose onto his feet, lifting them as he moved between her thighs, and she tipped her head back and moaned as his cock brushed her slick heat.

He answered her with a low moan of his own and seized her mouth again as he rocked between her thighs, rubbing himself up and down her cleft, driving her mad and making her breathless.

"Rath," she murmured, unable to hold back the plea as her need mounted, made her restless and pushed control beyond her grasp again.

His low groan stirred the heat in her veins, stoked the fire into an inferno that swept through her, burned all her reservations away and had her reaching between them and grasping his cock.

She was done with the teasing.

She grabbed his shoulder with her free hand and lifted herself, guided his blunt head down through her folds and moaned as it pushed inside her.

His entire body tensed.

He snarled, the raw and feral sound startling her.

And plunged deep inside her, filling her in one hard stroke that had a gasp bursting from her lips and her head flying back, her hands gripping his powerful shoulders and clinging to him.

He grunted and pressed her against the wall, held her there for a moment, his heart thundering against hers.

"I can't..." he muttered, his voice strained, and she shook her head, was right there with him, couldn't do this gently either, needed it too much.

She grabbed him by his jaw and kissed him hard, pressed her heels into his ass and spurred him on. He groaned, clutched her backside and thrust into her, slamming her against the wall with each powerful one, knocking the breath from her lungs.

She moaned and rocked her hips, writhing on his cock as pressure mounted, need rising higher still, until she was sure she was going to burst. Each long stroke of his cock had her sailing higher, her breath coming faster as he drove into her, sent waves of tingly heat cascading over her thighs and belly.

"Ivy," he grunted against her lips, his kiss as wild as his thrusts.

She buried her fingers in his hair and clung to him, kissed him hard, her tongue tangling with his, fighting him for dominance as she rocked on him, needing more.

He growled and twisted with her, pulled her away from the wall and planted her ass on the kitchen counter. She squeaked as he tugged her closer, slipped his arms beneath her knees and lifted her legs, spreading her. When he thrust this time, he went so deep she couldn't hold back the moan that exploded from her lips, savoured his answering one as he curled his hips and drove into her, his long cock filling her up and his pelvis brushing her sensitive bead with each meeting of their hips.

"Rath," she breathed, clutching him with both hands, heart thundering now, her body alive with sensation.

She wanted to tell him not to stop, that she was close, to keep doing what the fuck he was doing because she was going to scream if he didn't.

She screamed because he did.

It tore from her throat as every fibre of her being shattered into a thousand pieces and she threw her head back, arching her breasts against him as her entire body quaked, fire licking through her, tingles racing down her shaking thighs.

He grunted and kissed her neck as she clung to him, frozen in place, awash with sensation that overloaded her.

She couldn't move, could only stare at the hazy ceiling as he pumped her harder, faster, his breath hot on her skin as he licked and nipped at her neck, whispered her name against it and gripped her hard.

His big body tensed.

He bowed backwards as he bellowed her name, driving deep into her, his cock kicking, throbbing as his heat scalded her, and she moaned and shook as bliss swept through her again, the reaction so fierce it caught her off guard and left her breathless.

Rath held her as he breathed hard, muscles straining with each sharp exhalation, his body trembling against hers as he continued to pulse inside her.

The tension suddenly drained from his shoulders and he sagged over her, his fast breaths washing across her neck as he held her.

"Damn," he muttered against her throat and exhaled hard. "That was…"

"Yeah," she whispered, still right there with him as she drifted in a haze, every inch of her warm and sated, and she was sure she wouldn't be able to move for hours, was going to be floating for a while, completely useless to the world.

He peppered her throat with kisses as he pulled out of her, and as he bent over her, sweeping his mouth downwards towards her breasts, and another delicious shiver went through her, she amended her thoughts.

She could be useless later, after she'd had another taste of Rath.

He reached her breasts, swept his palms over the satin of her black bra, and pressed his thumbs into the edges of the cups. He groaned as he pushed them aside, popping her breasts free, and swooped on her right nipple.

Ivy moaned and thrust her breasts towards him as a hot shiver bolted through her, had need rising again as he kissed and licked her nipple, swirled his tongue around it and sucked the bead into his mouth, tugging on it.

Rath swept her back up into his arms and she wrapped her arms and legs around him as he carried her up the stairs, his lips not leaving her flesh, and his feet not missing a step. He dropped her on the soft sheets of his bed, covering her with his body, and continued his assault, driving her wild all over again.

His lips broke away from her breasts and she wanted to moan, wanted to complain, but then he kissed below them, forming a trail down her belly. She stretched her arms above her head and sank into the bed, anticipation coiling inside her, making her impatient as he lingered to swirl his tongue around her navel.

The first press of his mouth on her mound had her hips jacking up off the mattress. He laved his tongue over her flesh, each stroke sending shivers through her, making her breath come quicker, and she groaned and trembled as he wrapped his lips around her bead and suckled it, teased it with his teeth and then stroked it with his tongue again.

Ivy clutched the bedclothes, bunching them into her fists, and planted her feet on the mattress, unable to stop herself from lifting her hips and pressing herself into his mouth, urging him on.

He flicked his tongue over her pert nub. A hot shiver cascaded through her and over her thighs in response.

"Rath," she moaned, screwed her eyes shut and tipped her head back. "More."

He groaned and complied, swirled his tongue and flicked again, a faster stroke this time, one that had her hips shooting higher and need spiralling through her.

"More," she demanded, and fought the temptation to fondle her breasts, to tease her nipples to heighten her pleasure as he teased her with his mouth.

He found another way to heighten it for her.

He pressed two fingers into her core, sliding them as deep as he could get them before withdrawing them a little and rubbing her in just the right spot.

"Oh, God." She bit down on her lower lip, unsure she could survive such an assault.

Rath groaned and suckled her as he stroked her core.

Stars detonated across her eyes and she cried out as she broke apart, her body flexing around his fingers. He moaned again, slowed his strokes and lapped at her, and damn him, it only had her need mounting once more.

Ivy grabbed his hair and tugged, pulling him up to her.

He covered her body with his again, hooking her knees over his elbows and rubbing his hard length along her core as he kissed her, giving her what she needed.

She kept her right leg where it was as he lowered his hand, sighed as he eased his hips back and the tip of his cock penetrated her.

He held it there, just the head nudged inside her, and hooked his arm under her leg again, and then seemed to think the better of it. He released them both, lowered his body over hers, so his chest brushed her nipples, sending a fiery ache through her. He clutched her shoulder in his left hand, gripped her hip in his right and lifted it from the bed, and swallowed her moan in a kiss as he plunged into her, filling her again.

She kissed him hard as he drove into her, as fierce as before, his need flooding her, mingling with her own. He grunted as she clenched his cock, shuddered and pumped harder, and she moaned into his mouth. Each stroke of his length was divine, had her hips jacking higher, a need for him to go deeper rushing through her. She clung to him as she kissed him and writhed in his grip, the pressure building again, stealing control from her grasp.

Rath growled against her lips and loosed a low guttural surprised sound as his entire body jerked against her and his cock throbbed, pulsing hard, flooding her with jets of his seed. She moaned and quivered as she joined him, slumped beneath him and struggled to breathe as another release swept through her.

He groaned with each throb of her body around his, his shoulders shaking as she clung to them, and sagged against her. She sighed as he rolled onto his side, taking her with him, and wrapped his arms around her.

She wasn't sure how long they laid there, locked in each other's arms.

But as the delicious haze lifted, a trickle of fear went through her.
Fear she might have just made the biggest mistake of her life yet.
Not sleeping with Rath.
But falling in love with him.

CHAPTER 11

Rath stood on the deck, a mug of coffee warming his hand and keeping the morning chill off him as he stared at Ivy where she prowled the fringes of the trees by the river, stalking a male black bear.

He wasn't sure what to do.

He wasn't like the man who had hurt her, but sleeping with her might have been a mistake, not because he didn't like her, because he did.

Gods, he did.

It was because he couldn't let her stay, knew he had to make her leave today, before more cougars arrived, and that it was going to hurt her and she wouldn't understand. The alternative would produce the same results though. If she remained, and discovered what he was, what everyone who came to Cougar Creek was, she wouldn't understand then either.

Fuck, it hurt.

He rubbed the spot that burned the fiercest beneath his dark green fleece, right over his heart.

He didn't want to hurt her, didn't want that smile she had finally found again to be stolen from her by him, for her to suffer as she had when the man had treated her so callously.

Was he a bastard for wanting to send her away?

Absolutely.

But he had to protect her.

That need ran deep in his blood, in his soul, an urge he had to obey no matter what, because her safety came first.

It killed him that he wouldn't be able to give her a reason when he made her leave, because the only way to make her see the real reason she had to go was to tell her what was about to happen at the creek. How the fuck was he meant to explain a gathering of males coming to service the needs of females in heat?

No matter how he worded that, it would sound wrong to her, debauched, and would probably make her think he was fucking crazy, a delusional son of a bitch who had lost his mind out here in the wilderness.

Could he tell her that he wanted her to go and find the spirit bears?

A growl rumbled through him, not the first to peel from his lips this morning. The thought of her leaving tore at him, ripped at his strength and his heart, pulling him to pieces.

He could ask her to come back in a few weeks.

Would she?

Fuck. He scrubbed his free hand over his dark hair, tunnelled his fingers in the thick mass of it and growled again, the thought she might not come back, that he might never see her again, driving through him like a thousand spears, each sharper than the last, until he felt as if he was bleeding out.

Was going to die without her.

He paced the deck, his footfalls hard on the timbers, the energy boiling inside him impossible to contain. It needed an outlet or he was going to go insane, or worse.

His fragile control over his instincts as a male, *her* male, would snap and he would shift, his need to make her stay, to remain with him, forcing the reaction from him so he could dominate her and drive her into submission.

Her leaving was his fucking idea, so no damn way he was going to go cougar on her like that.

He stilled and looked across at her, a pained growl curling up his throat as his face crumpled, his heart growing heavy in his chest.

She couldn't go. He needed her too much.

Yesterday had shown him that, their moment of madness revealing something that he could no longer deny.

Ivy was his fated female.

His one true mate.

Rath watched her, aching to go to her, but afraid of it at the same time, because if he neared her, he would want to kiss her again, would want to keep kissing her until she agreed to be his.

It wasn't taboo to take a human mate. Many cougar shifters found their fated one outside of their species. He couldn't turn her, but bonding with her, mating with her, would extend her life by tying it to his.

They could live together.

He released a shuddering breath.

A fucking ridiculous dream.

The last time he had allowed himself to believe in forever, it had lasted only a decade before it had been taken from him, and it had left him jaded. Broken.

He couldn't believe in forever again, and he knew that if Ivy stayed, he would start wanting that with her.

He would fall in love with her.

If that happened and she ran when she discovered what he was, he would be more than broken.

The sensation of eyes on him rankled him, rousing his cougar side into a frenzy as a need to fight flooded him, and he tossed a black look in Storm's direction as his brother stepped out from the cover of the trees to his left, leaving the path to his cabin and the others on that side of the woods behind.

His brother drew his hand across his mouth, pretending to zip it shut.

Rath wasn't about to believe that promise. Sooner or later, Storm would bring up what had happened with Ivy yesterday, and her presence here at the creek, and his behaviour.

Still, he appreciated the reprieve as he breathed through the need to fight, quelling it again, because he needed time to get his head on straight where Ivy was concerned.

His gaze drifted back to her.

She tucked against a lodgepole pine, camera still trained on the bear where he drank from the river on the other side of it to her. He could feel her happiness, her excitement, and he ached at that, because he knew it stemmed from more than the fact she was doing what she loved.

He had a feeling she was coming to love it at the creek too, and maybe she was coming to love him.

He set his mug down on the small table and stepped off the deck.

He had to talk to her and it was going to be one hell of a tough conversation, but he had made up his mind.

His ears twitched, and he lifted his head and scanned the sky in all directions for the source of the sound.

A helicopter.

The bear spooked.

Alarm rang through him.

Rath signalled to his brother to go into hiding and had reached Ivy before she had even started to lower her camera. He swept her up into his arms and pulled her into the woods, pinning her to the trunk of a tree a few metres from the clearing.

He pressed his body against hers, covered her mouth with his right hand and looked down into her wide startled eyes as he whispered, "Keep still, and keep quiet."

He tilted his head back, tracking the helicopter as it drew closer, his heart pounding and adrenaline surging in his veins, rousing a powerful need to shift. Beneath his fleece, golden fur swept over his arms, and he struggled to stop the urge before his eyes changed and fangs lengthened, and Ivy saw what he was.

He wanted to break it to her gently, not scare the ever-living fuck out of her.

The chopper passed to his right, above the forest on the other side of the river, and drifted into the distance.

He loosed the breath he had been holding and eased his weight off Ivy as he leaned back to peer around the thick trunk of the tree. Across the clearing, Storm crouched near the riverside cabin, tucked against the tallest lodgepole pine.

Rath released Ivy's mouth.

"Why are you so tense?" she whispered, a trickle of fear flowing through her, and leaned to her right so she could look around the tree. "It was just a helicopter."

Rath snarled as his ears twitched again.

A chopper that was doubling back.

Fuck.

Wind whipped through the trees, shaking the branches and making them sway, kicking up leaf litter. The grass in the clearing was blasted flat as the helicopter hovered above it, and Storm crept back, sneaking further into the woods, his eyes on the sky.

Rath's heart thundered as the chopper eased down into the clearing, bumped as it landed and the blades wound down, whining as the pilot cut the engine.

His claws lengthened, canines elongating as a need to fight and protect his territory swept through him, and he kept his eyes off Ivy, afraid she would see the shift in his irises as they began to blaze gold.

Two men dressed in black fatigues exited the front of the chopper. Not hunters.

Or at least not the sort who were looking to shoot animals.

The need to fight grew stronger, pounding in his veins, stoked by the memories that assaulted him—a night that had taken almost everything from him.

One of the men opened the back right door of the pale gold chopper, and a handsome brunet male stepped out, his fine grey suit and polished black leather shoes out of place in the wilderness.

His dark eyes swung around the clearing.

Ivy stiffened.

Rath dropped his gaze to her.

"I know him," she whispered and glanced up at him. "It's Alexander... the man I sent the pictures to... but why is he here? *How* is he here?"

Questions Rath wanted answers to himself.

Ivy had only sent the photographs last night, not enough time for this bastard to use the landscape to identify the location of Cougar Creek.

"Get the guns," Alexander drawled, his English accent thick and regal, an arrogant tilt to his chin that had Rath wanting to punch it.

"He's after the bears!" Ivy lunged around the tree trunk.

Rath caught her arm, yanked her back to him and growled as he shoved her against the tree. "Don't move."

Because he would lose his shit if this male saw her and targeted her.

"I have to stop him." She struggled against him. "I don't know how he found this place. He was meant to be in England. How the hell is he here?"

"I intend to ask him about that," Rath snarled.

She paled, her hazel eyes enormous as her fine dark eyebrows furrowed. "Oh, Rath... I didn't tell him, I swear. I'm so sorry. I'm so—"

He cut her off with a brief kiss, smoothed his palms over her cheeks and held her face as he lingered, wanting to reassure her, and needing the contact to calm himself and to give him the strength to do what he needed to do.

Hunters had almost succeeded in taking everything from him once and it wasn't going to happen again. He wasn't going to lose Ivy, or his brother. It wasn't going to happen. He would keep them both safe. He would.

"I know, Sweetheart," he murmured against her lips and stole another kiss. "Stay here."

He reluctantly released her, sucked down a deep steadying breath and strode out into the clearing.

He had to protect his kin.

He had to protect her.

No matter the cost.

CHAPTER 12

Ivy couldn't breathe as Rath walked out from beneath the trees and towards the helicopter and Alexander. The instant the men in black combat gear noticed him, they lifted their assault rifles and took aim. Her heart skipped a beat and lodged in her throat.

She clung to the rough bark of the tree, shaking so hard she feared letting go, sure she would collapse into a heap.

Rath.

Beneath his green fleece, his shoulders tensed, and cold swept through her when she realised it wasn't fear that had him coiling tight.

He meant to fight.

He didn't stand a chance against two armed men.

A need shot through her, lit her up and drove her to break cover.

A need to protect him.

She set her camera down on the roots of the tree and stormed out of the woods on weak legs that only seemed to grow weaker as she broke cover. Her eyes locked on Alexander, her eyebrows knitted hard above them as she clenched her fists at her sides. As she glared at him, anger rose to overwhelm her fear and put strength in her step, fury that he had dared to use her twice now.

Well she was damned if she was going to let him hurt the bears.

She was damned if she would let him hurt Rath.

Rath tilted his head to his right and frowned at her as she reached him, his golden eyes dark. He could shout at her later for disobeying him, right now she was more concerned with saving his ass.

"You can't shoot the bears, Alexander," she snapped and stopped a step in front of Rath, placing herself in the firing line.

Rath seized her arm and pulled her back, his grip fierce and unyielding as he moved to shield her with his big body.

Ivy tried to get free, but he refused to release her, kept her hidden behind him no matter what she did. The urge to snap at him too faded when she felt him trembling. He was afraid now.

Because she had placed herself in danger?

Alexander wouldn't let the men hurt her. He was a bastard, but not that much of one.

She touched Rath's hand. "Let me talk with him."

Rath looked over his right shoulder at her, his rugged face filled with fury, but his eyes flooded with concern, worry for her. She stroked his hand and smiled softly, wanting to reassure him. Some of the tension eased from his body and he drew her up beside him, but didn't release her.

Because he feared she would go to Alexander?

No damn way.

She had been angry with him when he had hurt her, but now she hated him. The thought that he had used her, and was likely using the other photographers he funded, to find a location to go hunting sickened her, and she was going to let him have both barrels.

"You can't shoot the bears here, Alexander," she snapped, her pulse pounding again as her anger rose back to the fore, the thought of the mother bear or the male she had photographed today being targeted and killed pouring fury through her veins. "It's illegal."

He arched a dark eyebrow at that and moved a step closer, coming to stand between his two lackies.

Rath's hand tensed against her wrist.

She glanced at him, but he hadn't taken his eyes off Alexander, was staring him down in a way that made it clear he wanted to fight him, and he would if it came to it.

Hell, she didn't want it to come to it. The thought of Rath fighting these men terrified her. Even if his brother helped, they would still be at a huge disadvantage. She hadn't spotted any rifles in Rath's cabin. There was no way they could win against the guns the men had without weapons of their own.

She had to defuse the situation before it got that far.

"I don't know how you found me," she bit out, "but I won't let you do this. If I had known you wanted to hunt bears, I never would have taken your money."

Alexander merely glanced at her, his dark eyes devoid of emotion, and held his right hand out to the man beside him. A man who moved to the chopper and came back with another black assault rifle.

He placed it into Alexander's hand, and the bastard casually checked it was loaded, looked pleased when it was to his satisfaction, and had the audacity to smile at her.

"It was easy to find you. I have a tracker sewn into the lining of your backpack. I've been following your movements for months now."

She felt sick at that. "You've been tracking me all this time? Why?"

He lowered the weapon to his side. "Because I am hunting. I have several people like you out here, desperate little photographers who will take pictures and send them back to me, covering a far wider area than I could by myself."

Son of a bitch.

She lunged towards him. "I won't let you hurt the bears!"

Rath pulled her on her wrist, and she banged into him, her back to his chest. She huffed and yanked her arm free, her anger getting the better of her, the thought of anyone controlling her pushing her to lash out, and she didn't want to lash out at Rath.

She wanted to pummel Alexander's smug face into a bloody pulp.

Rath's eyes tracked her, intense and focused, sending a warm shiver through her. She held herself together and refused to give in to the urge to attack Alexander, because Rath would try to protect her, and would end up caught in the crossfire, and she didn't want to see him hurt.

She didn't want him to fight.

"I am not here to hunt bears," Alexander said, his casual tone grating on her last nerve.

"Why are you here then? What's with the guns if you're not hunting?" She folded her arms across her chest and stared him down, waiting for him to explain himself and hoping he got the message that she was on to him and wasn't going to let him get away with whatever he had planned.

"Oh, I am hunting." He smiled slowly as his eyes shifted to Rath. "I am here to hunt cougar."

Ivy didn't understand. She hadn't sent him any pictures that revealed there were cougars in this location. Rath had mentioned they lived in these parts, but then they lived across the entire region. Her pictures of the bears shouldn't have alerted Alexander to the fact the big cats lived in this valley in particular. She definitely hadn't spotted any signs of them along the river, which meant she hadn't accidentally photographed something that revealed they were here.

"You need to leave," Rath snarled and spread his feet shoulder-width apart, his entire body coiling like a spring as she looked at him. "Before things get ugly for you."

They were going to get ugly for Rath if she didn't do something.

She had to protect him.

Ivy pushed past him, placing herself between Rath and Alexander, closer to the bastard she was going to make leave. "I'll call the authorities if you don't leave now, Alexander. There are no cougars here, and it's illegal to hunt them outside of the season anyway."

He kept his dark eyes pinned on Rath.

"There are cougars here, Ivy." He lowered his gaze to her, and she shivered as hers met it and the coldness in it hit her hard together with his words. "You just haven't realised it yet."

Realised what?

"One has been right in front of you all this time," he drawled.

She looked over her shoulder at Rath.

Shrieked as Alexander grabbed her and twisted her in his arms, banding his left one across her chest and pinning her arms to her breasts. She kicked at him, pushed and scrabbled, trying to break free as a vicious snarl echoed around her, a sound that sent a chill skating down her spine and had her wild eyes searching for the cougar who had made it.

But there was only Rath before her.

The cold touch of metal against her temple had her freezing, her heart lodging in her throat and lungs squeezing tight.

"Ivy," Rath rasped, a pained expression crossing his face before it twisted into a savage sneer. "Let her go."

When he signalled with his left hand, her eyes widened. His brother. Storm had to be watching events unfold. Judging by the way Rath kept his eyes off the spot behind Alexander, where the riverside cabin was, his brother was there, protecting Ember and her mother.

"I've spent a long time trying to find this place." Alexander pressed the gun harder against her temple, forcing her to tilt her head, and she refused to let the tears that burned the backs of her eyes line her lashes.

Rath glanced at her, pain and fear flashing in his golden eyes, and then only darkness as they landed back on Alexander. "I said, let her go."

Alexander ignored him. "All I had to go on were the reports I found in my grandfather's study after he died... faded photographs taken during reconnaissance missions before the main mission launched. I found that place, and you weren't there."

Missions?

What the hell was Alexander talking about?

"Just let me go." She struggled against him and managed to push his arm away from her chest an inch.

He tightened it around her, lowered his head and breathed against her neck. "Don't make me hurt you, Ivy. I do hate having to hurt beautiful women."

That growl came again, fiercer this time, and Alexander chuckled low in his throat.

"You want her, don't you?" Alexander pressed a kiss to her neck and she squirmed, wriggling away from his touch.

This time, the growl was more of a snarl, a low feral sound that held a note of warning in it and had her tensing, ready for the beast to attack her.

She looked for the source of it.

Her eyes locked with Rath's bright golden ones.

His lips twisted in a sneer that flashed unusually sharp canines. "I thought you looked familiar. You're as ugly as the bastard who led the attack on us that night. It's a shame the fucker fled when shit went bad... didn't have the balls to stick around and finish the job."

Alexander tensed behind her and she could feel him shaking, trembling with anger.

Rath smiled slowly. "Left in a chopper... ditching the survivors... after I left my mark on him."

"It took him months and countless surgeries to recover from that wound," Alexander barked.

Rath growled, "It took my kin decades to recover from the scars Archangel left on us, and we're still recovering from it now. Your family took everything from me... they took my parents... they took my wife and my unborn kid."

A cold shiver swept down Ivy's spine and her breath seized in her lungs.

Before she could gather her wits and ask what the hell they were all talking about, speaking of decades and Archangel, and what sounded like a battle to her, Alexander spoke.

"You killed my father."

Rath snorted at that. "He only got what he deserved for killing so many of my kind and stealing others to take back to your sick fucking laboratories in England to 'study' and 'document' as if they were animals."

"You *are* animals!" Alexander's grip on her tightened further, squeezing her ribs and making it hard to breathe.

"We're not animals," Rath barked and advanced a step, didn't back down when the two men tensed and moved their fingers to rest over the triggers on the assault rifles they had aimed at him. "We're not like you either. We were peaceful... and you came to our home and attacked us. We defended ourselves."

His stormy golden eyes fell to her and narrowed, sending another wave of cold through her.

Together with his words.

"Were you aware your sponsor is a sick son of a bitch who hunts people like me?"

Her ears rang.

Numbness crashed over her.

She whispered, "He hunts people?"

The cold press of the gun against her temple had that hitting her hard, and her knees turned to rubber, threatening to buckle. She locked them as anger swept through her, so hot and fierce it burned away the chill of shock. She wrestled against Alexander.

Froze when he moved his hand to her throat and squeezed it hard, his fingertips digging into her skin.

"I hunt creatures who mean to harm us," he snarled and tugged her closer to him, pressed his cheek to hers and tilted her head up, forcing her to look at Rath. "That isn't a man standing in front of you... it isn't a man you obviously invited between your legs and feel something for."

His low chuckle left her cold again.

"Maybe I'll make a test subject of you... see what comes out when a human is impregnated by a monster... since you obviously enjoy fucking them."

"I didn't enjoy fucking you, and you're clearly a monster," she bit out and elbowed him in the ribs.

Alexander spun her away from him and slammed the butt of the rifle into her left cheek, the blow sending stars spinning across her vision, edging it with black. She hit the grass, head twirling and throbbing.

Something growled again.

"You alright?" Rath snarled and she struggled to look at him.

He wobbled in her vision.

His golden eyes glowing as he stared Alexander down.

Alexander chuckled. "I wanted to kill you, wanted you to pay for taking my father from me when I found you... but now... now I think I'll take both of you with me."

Her head turned and she pressed a hand to it, grimaced at the heat that bloomed beneath her fingers, wetness that had her stomach lurching.

Alexander smiled down at her.

"Archangel will enjoy studying you and the child you'll produce for them."

CHAPTER 13

"Archangel will enjoy studying you and the child you'll produce for them."

It was the last straw for Rath.

He burst towards the male to the right of Ivy, nearest the helicopter, and grabbed his assault rifle, tugging it up as the male became aware of him and began to wrestle to get the weapon out of his grip.

Rath twisted the gun, elbowed him in the face and turned the weapon on Alexander.

His finger squeezed the trigger, the angle awkward but effective as bullets sprayed and Alexander dived away from Ivy, rolling across the grass towards the helicopter and behind the male fighting Rath for his weapon. The bastard shoved forwards, kicking the barrel of the gun up towards the sky, and knocking Rath back.

The second soldier took aim and Rath leaped backwards, avoiding the bullets that whizzed towards him, barely missing him and the male he had been fighting. He pressed his left boot into the ground and kicked right, sprinted around the back of the chopper and used it as cover as his heart thundered and fur swept over his skin beneath his fleece, a need to shift bolting through him as Ivy shrieked.

"Get off me!"

A masculine grunt sounded and Ivy appeared in view, crab-crawling backwards across the grass, her hazel eyes wide and her terror striking him hard.

"Run," he snarled when she looked at him, fear flashing in her eyes.

Fear for him.

Blood tracked down the left side of her head and he growled at the sight of it, couldn't hold back the vicious sound as anger blazed through him and a need to fight swamped him, a hunger to avenge her and make these humans pay for what they had done to her.

She twisted onto her front and scrambled across the grass, heading for cover.

Alexander gave chase.

Rath snarled and kicked off, but a hail of bullets had him diving back behind the cover of the chopper, and he could only watch as she tried to evade the male chasing her.

Fuck.

Storm came out of nowhere and slammed into Alexander's back, lifting him off the ground as he grappled with him, pulling him back. He tossed the male onto the grass and leaped on him. The two males turned towards their boss as he grunted, and Rath growled as he launched at the one nearest to him.

He grabbed the male's weapon again and yanked it towards him, and the male made a strangled sound as the strap cut into his neck. He slammed his right fist into the hunter's face—once, twice, and a third time—and the male staggered and slumped, the strap slipping free of his head as he dropped.

Rath turned the weapon on the other hunter and fired.

The male was quick to react, sprayed bullets at him as he hurled himself to his left and skidded across the grass.

Not quick enough though.

The hunter howled as a bullet tore through his leg, clutched it and clawed across the grass, heading for the chopper. Rath took aim.

Storm bellowed in agony.

He twisted towards his brother and snarled when he saw the blood flowing down his right arm from a slash in his black hoody and the flash of a blade in Alexander's grasp. The male lunged with the knife again and Ivy screamed like a banshee as she barrelled into Storm and shoved him, pushing him clear of the attack.

"Run," Rath barked again, because he needed her away from danger, but she ignored him and grabbed Storm, trying to pull him away from Alexander.

Storm growled and swatted at her, was on his feet the moment she released him and ready to launch back at Alexander.

Alexander was on his feet though, running for the helicopter as the engines began to wind up.

Who the fuck was still inside?

All three males were still out in the clearing, the one he had wounded staggering into an upright position, leaning heavily on his rifle and using it as a crutch, and the other one still out cold on the grass.

He glanced at the chopper, caught a flash of a blonde female leaning over the pilot's seat, and then threw himself flat as his senses screamed a warning at him. Bullets zipped over his head and he rolled as Alexander lowered his aim, adjusting it. They tore through the grass, sending the scent of earth into the air, and Rath growled as he found his feet and sprang at the male.

Storm beat him to it again, only this time, it wasn't in his human form.

Fuck.

Rath swiftly checked on Ivy, and sure enough, she sat on her backside on the grass, her skin pale and eyes round as she stared at the huge golden cougar that slammed into Alexander and knocked him sideways.

The female in the chopper shrieked as the bullets ripped through the metal and shattered glass, and smoke poured from below the rotor blades.

The male he had knocked out groaned as he came around, and the one he had injured took aim at Rath's brother.

Damn. He couldn't let Storm fight alone, and his brother was right, they would have the advantage in their cougar forms.

Besides, there was no point in holding back now Ivy had seen Storm shift.

Rath pulled off his fleece and t-shirt, kicked out of his boots and tore open his jeans. He growled as he shifted, his bones lengthening or contracting, transforming beneath his skin as golden fur swept over his arms and legs, and down his back, and a band of white fur rippled down his chest.

He felt Ivy's eyes on him, her shock as she watched him turn from a man into a huge cougar, and he wanted to cry at her, to call to her and have her come to him even when he knew she wouldn't.

Not now.

Not ever.

She would run as soon as he gave her the chance, and she would never look back.

He couldn't hold back the low moan of mourning that rolled through him, let the pain swamp him for only a second but it tore him apart. He shut it down and launched at the male he had knocked out, taking him back down. He clawed at the male's chest, savaging him as he grunted and wrestled with him, desperately trying to push his weight off him.

The other male hollered something and Rath sprang backwards as he fired, leaping high into the air. The bullets tore through the hunter instead, and he gargled as blood leaked from the holes in his chest and from the corners of his lips.

"Shit." The male swung the gun up as Rath landed, aiming it at him.

Storm snarled as he leaped on the male, front legs open and paws spread wide. The male turned and grunted as the full weight of Storm landed on him, and then screamed as his brother brought his head down and tore into his throat.

Alexander shoved to his feet, clutching his side, crimson slipping from between his fingers, and grabbed a gun from the grass. He lifted it, his eyes cold as he turned them on Ivy.

Rath's heart froze in his chest.

"I was wrong... the way to make you suffer..." The male slid his gaze towards Rath. "I'll take everything you love from you and then I'll put you in a cage to rot."

Alexander's finger squeezed the trigger.

Rath roared as he kicked off, sailed through the air as Ivy gasped and recoiled, trying to flee, and grunted as the bullet meant for her tore into his right shoulder. He hit the grass hard, tumbled across it as the fiery heat that ripped through him forced him to shift back, and landed face down, breathing hard as agony rolled through him, the pain so intense that he couldn't move.

He had to move.

Ivy was still in danger.

He heard Storm growl and Alexander grunt as his brother attacked him, and pushed his hands into the grass, forced himself to move so he could help his brother protect Ivy.

He wouldn't fail her.

The urge was strong, had him moving despite the debilitating pain that screamed through him with every flex of his right arm. He snarled as he lumbered onto his feet and twisted towards Alexander where he was backing away from Storm, struggling to evade his brother's swipes of his claws as Storm hissed and growled at him, and sprang away whenever Alexander opened fire.

A hail of bullets forced Storm to leap further away, leaving Alexander a clear path to Ivy.

The bastard raised his gun and aimed it at her again, his grin cold as she shook her head, her fear hitting Rath hard.

He squeezed the trigger again.

The gun just clicked.

Alexander looked down at it, his eyes slowly widening.

Rath roared as he barrelled into him and slammed him into the ground, sending the gun clattering across the grass as it tumbled from his grip. He snarled as he pinned Alexander beneath him and smashed his right fist into the bastard's face, knocking his head to his left. Satisfaction rolled through him as the male grunted, blood coating his lower lip, and he struck him again, and again, his fury getting the better of him.

When the male went still, he sagged forwards and breathed hard, blood streaming down his right arm, the pain returning as his anger faded and the knowledge that Ivy was safe washed through him, easing the hold his instincts had on him.

He wavered and lumbered onto his feet, staggered back a few steps as he clutched his arm, his heart racing and breath sawing from his lips.

"What do you want me to do with this?" Storm's deep voice rolled over him, had him lifting his head and trying to focus on him as his brother moved on the edge of his vision.

A slim blonde dressed in a grey pencil skirt and white blouse hung from Storm's hand, his grip on her arm so tight the skin around his fingers had blanched.

"Lock her in one of the cabins until we can question her." Rath's words came out slurred and he frowned as the world around him wobbled.

"Rath?" Ivy's soft voice came from his left, a soothing balm in his ringing ears.

He looked at her.

And passed out.

CHAPTER 14

Things had taken a turn towards crazy.

But as Rath went down, the fact he wasn't human, the shocking revelation that he could shift into a wild animal, and the knowledge he'd had a wife once and had lost her and part of his family to humans who wanted to hunt him and hurt him, didn't matter.

All that mattered was saving him.

Ivy sank to her knees beside him on the torn up grass, pulled him onto his back and gasped at the sight of him. Blood drenched his right side, leaking from a hole in his shoulder.

"Rath," she breathed, patted his cheek and tried to rouse him, but he remained deathly still.

Everything Yasmin had taught her leaped to the front of her mind and she automatically removed her hoody, bundled it up and pressed it to the wound to stem the flow of blood. Her friend had trained her in tackling most injuries, wanting her to be prepared and know how to deal with them should she injure herself while alone in the wilderness. She doubted Yasmin had been expecting her to use that knowledge on another.

On a man who could change into a cougar.

She kept pressure on the wound as she scanned the full length of his body, searching for any other injuries that might place him in danger. There were only cuts and bruises. She looked back at her bloodied hands where they pressed into the dark fabric, and then at his face. He was pale, beads of sweat dotting his brow, his lips slack.

Fuck, he looked like death and she hated it.

"Come on, Rath," she murmured and pressed the fingers of her free hand to his throat, heart pounding a sickening rhythm against her chest, her breath seizing in her lungs as she searched him for a sign of life.

Time seemed to stretch into an eternity before she finally found a pulse.

It was strong.

Fast.

"Motherfucker." Storm's deep voice made her jump, and she swiftly twisted to face him.

He had transformed into a cougar too, and had been as naked as a jaybird when he had walked away with a stunned blonde in tow, obeying his brother's command. Thankfully, he'd had the decency to put his trousers back on at least.

He crouched beside Rath, a wealth of concern in his grey eyes.

Eyes that matched Rath's so perfectly it brought tears to hers.

The fear she had been fighting pressed down on her. Not fear of Rath, or what he and his brother were, but fear that she was going to lose him.

Part of her felt she should be afraid of him, but she felt as drawn to him now as she had been before she had discovered he wasn't like her.

She still couldn't believe he could transform into a cougar.

Or the fact he had protected her, had saved her life by taking a bullet for her and had killed Alexander.

Ivy looked across at Alexander as Storm went into action, hauling his brother into his arms and over his shoulder, his words lost on her as she stared at the bastard who had come here to hurt them.

Kill them.

Her gut twisted as she looked at his body.

She was sure she should have been shocked or horrified by what Rath had done to him too, should feel bad about it, guilty for her part in it, but it had been him or them, and all she felt was relieved that he was dead.

"Ivy," Storm snapped, dragging her back to him. "I'm going to need your help."

She nodded, pushed onto her feet and clutched her soiled hoody to her chest as she followed Storm to Rath's cabin, trying to shut out the ache in her temple as it began to build again, reminding her that Rath wasn't the only one who had been injured. Her own wound could wait. Rath came first.

Storm set his brother down on the wooden floor and she stared down at Rath as he went into the bathroom.

When he emerged and dumped several white towels, bandages and other items next to his brother, she startled from her stupor and pushed away from her fear.

She wasn't going to lose Rath.

She moved to his right side, nudging his brother aside, and dropped to her knees. Her hand slipped on the fresh blood on Rath's shoulder when she tried to lift him, his dead weight working against her.

Storm crouched and grabbed his brother, lifting him for her, and she thanked him with a nod, and peered beneath Rath's shoulder.

"No exit wound." She tried to remember what Yasmin had told her about treating bullet wounds, and wished her friend was here with her now, because she was sure Yasmin could handle this without breaking a sweat, would have Rath patched up and back on his feet in no time.

"We need to get the bullet out." Storm waited for her to place a folded towel beneath Rath's shoulder before lowering his brother onto it.

He straightened, stepped over his brother's head, and rifled through the drawers in the kitchen in front of her. A knife flashed in his hand when he turned to face her and her stomach lurched.

She must have paled, because Storm smiled tightly.

"We just need to open the wound a little." He kneeled beside his brother's head and glanced at her, concern lighting his grey eyes, making them more blue. "I hope you have a strong stomach."

Those words told her what he wouldn't, revealed her purpose to her and she swallowed hard, bracing herself against what she was about to do.

"I don't have anything else we can use." Storm's voice dripped with an apology.

Ivy shook her head. "It's fine. I can do it. Yasmin showed me what to do."

Although, the thought of sticking her fingers into Rath's wound and seeking the bullet had her stomach churning and bile rising up her throat.

"I'll have to thank this Yasmin sometime." Storm gave her another tight smile and then his handsome face shifted into a pained grimace as he looked at his brother. "I fucking hope you stay unconscious for this... and I'm sorry."

Ivy looked away the moment the knife pierced the wound, covered her mouth as the scent of blood in the air grew thicker, and her mind filled with images of Storm cutting his brother, not letting her escape the gruesome sight.

Storm dropped the knife and pressed a towel to the wound, muttering dark things to himself.

She drew down several deep breaths, dragging her courage a little higher with each one, feeling Storm's eyes on her as he waited.

Ivy nodded.

He moved.

She glanced at Rath, just enough to make sure her fingers hit their target, and balked as slick heat surrounded them, his flesh giving way as she pressed her fingers into the wound.

"Breathe," she whispered to herself, swallowed and closed her eyes, pressed deeper and ignored how her stomach lurched when a wet sucking sound broke the silence.

She was going to throw up.

"You're doing great," Storm murmured, voice soft and gentle, encouraging. "As soon as the bullet is out, he'll be able to start healing the wound. He'll heal fast, Ivy. You just need to get the bullet out."

She nodded, sucked down another breath to stop herself from vomiting and probed deeper. Bile shot up her throat when she felt bone, the jagged end of it scraping her fingertip, and she braced her other hand against the floor, sure she would throw up this time.

Storm moved behind her and gently rested his hand on her shoulder. "Take a break if you need it."

She shook her head. "Something is broken."

"He'll heal it, I swear. We don't break so easily. You can't keep a good cougar down." He rubbed her shoulder, palming it softly.

Ivy nodded again and pushed past the broken bone, and grimaced as her knuckles hit his flesh, and the reason Storm had sliced the wound open wider made a sickening sort of sense. She pressed forwards, her ring and little finger sinking into the wound, allowing her to reach deeper with her other two fingers.

Where the hell was that bullet?

She stilled as her fingers brushed something and it moved. She twisted her hand, her eyes widening as she felt it was small, jagged in places, and moved freely. Definitely not part of his body. She opened her fingers like scissors and hoped she wasn't doing any damage as she fumbled with the bullet, trying to get hold of it.

Her breath lodged in her throat as she managed to get it between her two fingers, and her heart slammed hard against her chest as she carefully pulled her fingers up, her body trembling as she tried not to drop it.

"You're doing great," Storm murmured again. "Almost there."

She wasn't sure, because she couldn't look, the thought of seeing her fingers in the wound too much to bear, let alone actually seeing them.

Cool air washed over her fingers, helping her judge how far she had come.

When they pulled free of Rath's flesh with a sickening sucking sound, she sank back on her hip and brought her hand in front of her. Crimson covered it, but she shut out the sight of it, her focus on the piece of metal between her fingers.

It looked so small, so harmless, but it had almost caused more damage than she could bear.

It had almost taken Rath from her.

Storm pressed the towel back against his brother's shoulder as she looked down at Rath and let the bullet fall from her fingers.

"Ivy." Storm's soft tone had her looking at him. "Stay... and give him a chance to explain when he comes around."

She nodded, wanting to ease him, because she had no intention of going anywhere, not until Rath was better at least.

Not until she knew what crazy world she had wandered into at Cougar Creek.

"What did you do with Gabriella?" She studied Storm's face for a sign that he had hurt the woman, hoping that he hadn't and that he didn't intend to either.

"That her name?" He frowned at her, sandy eyebrows dropping low above his grey eyes.

"She's Alexander's half-sister... but she's a good woman, Storm."

She could see where he got his name as his eyes darkened and his face followed them.

"I can't trust your judge of character," he bit out. "You thought that hunter bastard was a good man too."

It was true, so she let him off for snapping at her.

He looked down at his brother, huffed and pushed onto his feet. "Stay with him. I'll be back soon."

She wanted to stop him, because she knew he was going to see Gabriella, but when she opened her mouth to say something, the way he stopped in the doorway and glared over his shoulder at her made her think the better of it.

He wouldn't hurt Gabriella.

Rath wanted to question her, and she doubted Storm would risk her clamming up by hurting her before his brother had a chance to speak with her, which meant she had time to convince Rath that Gabriella was innocent.

Or at least she hoped Gabi was.

Ivy had only met her a handful of times, and she had never seemed interested in Alexander's business, but she had been travelling with her brother. Had things changed? God, she hoped they hadn't and Gabriella was an innocent caught up in things beyond her understanding not someone who was now working for the same organisation as Alexander had been.

She stared at the door, getting the sinking feeling that it wouldn't matter to Storm if Gabi wasn't involved in Archangel, because she shared Alexander's blood in part, and his family had been responsible for the terrible things that had happened to Storm's family all those decades ago.

He was going to want revenge.

Would Rath want it too?

Ivy returned her focus to Rath, pushing out her concern for Gabi because he needed it more. She set to work closing the wound as best she could with what she had and bandaging it, and cleaned some of his other injuries, covering them with dressings. When her work was done, she took a cushion from the couch, placed it under his head, and covered him with a blanket.

She turned the armchair near him around and sat in it, her eyes locked on him as she tucked her legs up to her chest and waited. Time trickled past, his breathing levelling out and a little colour returning to his cheeks. The day wore on, the sun moving across the mountains, and Storm came at some point to drop off her camera and pack, and check on his brother.

It was close to evening when she finally moved, using the bathroom and then filling the kettle with water. She made herself a coffee, and as she turned, she found Rath watching her, a hazy edge to his golden eyes.

She set her mug down, picked up a pitcher of water and poured him a glass, and kneeled beside his head.

"I can't believe you're still here," he croaked.

Ivy helped him sit up a little, wincing at the same time as he did, and brought the glass to his lips. "I didn't know anything about what Alexander was involved in... about what he wanted... or about... you. I swear."

He swallowed the water and eased back on a sigh, his eyes on the ceiling. "I know."

"I didn't know anything about what happened to you and your family either. I'm sorry." She set the glass down beside her and dropped her hands into her lap, her eyes on him even though he kept his locked away from her, as if he couldn't bring himself to look at her.

"You don't need to apologise," he murmured and closed his eyes. "It's in the past now... and while I still feel a sense of loss... I no longer remember what she looked like. I only have vague memories and feelings from time to time."

Ivy steeled herself, her heart stinging at the thought of him with another woman, one he had clearly loved, had mourned and part of him still mourned.

"How long ago did you lose her?" She looked down at her knees, bracing herself for the answer, sure it would deliver another shock to her that would tilt her world even more off its axis.

Rath let out a long sigh. "Thirty-six years ago."

Her eyes widened. Two years before she had been born.

She lifted her gaze to Rath, but he kept his eyes closed, shutting her out. Why? Because he didn't want to tell her these things? Or because he feared how she would react?

"How... how old are you?" Her heart pounded again, a strange airy sensation flowing through her, making her feel as if she was floating, dreaming all of this.

He grimaced. "One hundred and forty-eight."

Wow. She swallowed hard at that, stared wide-eyed at him, trying to make herself believe he was telling her the truth. What reason did he have to lie to her? If he had wanted to lie, he would have told her he had lost his wife only a few years ago and that he was the age he looked—somewhere in his late thirties.

Ivy could only stare at him as she worked to make that slowly sink in. Rath was almost one hundred and fifty years old, was a century and then some older than she was, and had fought in some sort of battle before she had been born.

"Who is Archangel?" And why would they want to study someone like Rath, or use her in such a sick way?

"Hunters." His voice cracked, and he struggled to clear his throat. He grimaced as he coughed, his right arm twitching, hand flexing.

She picked up the glass of water, lifted his head and placed it to his lips again, held it there as he drank deep, draining the glass. When he was done, she eased him back down onto the pillow and went to stand.

Shock whipped through her when he seized her wrist with his right hand, not letting her move away, a low growl on his lips.

His eyes widened slightly when he looked at his hand, surprise flashing in them, and he released her and sank back against the pillow. Blood bloomed on the bandages over his gunshot wound.

"Sorry," he croaked. "I'm... I..."

He turned his face away from her.

He didn't need to tell her the reason he had reacted, had stopped her from moving away from him. She could feel it in him, and that was stranger than anything she had seen yet.

She had panicked him by going to move away and he had reacted on instinct, needing to keep her near to him, because he feared she was going to leave.

"You were telling me about Archangel," she prompted gently as she eased back onto her knees beside him, showing him that she wasn't going anywhere.

Nothing he told her could scare her away.

She had seen what he was, and while it had shocked her at the time, she wasn't afraid of him.

When he didn't speak, she filled the silence, hoping to reassure him.

"I've travelled the world as a photographer." She shifted onto her backside and crossed her legs. "In South America, when I was looking for jaguars in the Pantanal, I met a tribe who worshipped them and believed they transformed into humans during certain times of the year."

She had thought it local folklore until today though.

When Rath edged his head towards her an inch, she continued.

"I met a holy man in India who spoke of tigers devouring human souls so they can walk in our world." She had figured him for an eccentric determined to sweep her up in his story to charm some money off her, a tourist in his eyes.

She looked at Rath, canting her head to her right as she took him in and remembered the incredible sight of him transforming into a huge sleek cougar.

"So maybe it isn't so crazy that you can change appearance… maybe you're one of those shapeshifters the people I met spoke of with reverence."

He closed his eyes. "I'm not a jaguar, or a tiger. They're a pride species."

The way he spoke of them told her that there were other shapeshifters out there in the world, and the tribe and the holy man were right to believe in them.

"You have a pride." She tucked her knees against her chest. "Storm, and the others here."

He frowned. "We're solitary creatures in reality, but at times, we act as a pride."

She recalled him saying he was a solitary kind of guy, and that he couldn't understand why people liked cities, and now that aspect of his personality made a lot of sense to her. She knew cougars, had done her research into them before, when she had debated tracking them to photograph them a few years ago. They preferred to keep to themselves, but would tolerate other cougars at certain times, especially during winter when food was scarce, going so far as to share it with other cougars who had shown them the same kindness.

"Is a cougar your only form?" When he looked at her, a line forming between his dark eyebrows as they dipped low, she added, "Other than this one."

He nodded, grimaced and rubbed at his shoulder with his left hand.

Ivy leaned over and caught his wrist, stopping him. "You'll aggravate it. We had nothing to sew it with, but your brother assured me it would heal once I got the bullet out."

His grey eyes widened and zipped to her. "You removed the bullet?"

She rolled her shoulders. "I have a friend who's a doctor… an overprotective friend. She insisted on training me in all aspects of field medicine, just in case."

Her eyes dropped to her hand on his wrist and she couldn't stop herself from stroking her thumb over his skin as her thoughts weighed her down, the tempest of feelings she had been swept up in just hours ago swirling through her again, fear of losing Rath at the front of them.

"You'll really heal?" She kept her eyes on her hand, afraid of looking at him as she asked that, although she wasn't sure why. Because he might tell her that he wouldn't? Because he might see in her eyes that she needed him to heal, that he had frightened her and part of her was still convinced she was going to lose him?

He grunted, clenched his jaw and brought his right hand up, placing it over hers. "I will, Ivy... you don't have to worry about me. I'm strong."

She nodded and blew her breath out on a strained chuckle. "I'm still finding it hard to fathom everything that just happened. Suddenly the man I'm... you're a cougar... and Alexander is trying to kill me... and everything no longer makes sense."

"It makes sense," he husked and closed his fingers over her hand, holding it to him. "It might take a while for it to sink in, but you know it makes sense, Ivy."

She took her hand from his and sank back on her bottom again. "Should I feel bad that we killed him? I feel as if I should."

He growled and grimaced as he twisted towards her, propping himself up on his left elbow. "You have nothing to feel guilty about. I killed him. It had nothing to do with you."

"But it did." She caught the shock that flitted across his handsome face as her eyes met his. "You killed him because of me... because he threatened me."

He looked as if he wanted to deny that, but no words left his lips. He just stared at her in silence before lowering his gaze to the floor, and then looking off to her left, towards the door.

"I wanted to kill him," he whispered, his deep voice laced with anger. "I vowed the night his grandfather and father attacked my pride that all in his bloodline would pay for what they had done."

His grey eyes drifted back to her, filled with warmth and something else, something she felt sure was fear.

"When he... the thought of you... I couldn't stop myself."

She had felt that in him when he had been pinning Alexander. She had felt his fury, his need to protect her, how it had driven him despite his injuries, had made him hurt himself in order to keep her safe.

"I know," she whispered and lifted her hand, stroked it over the bandages across his right shoulder, her eyes on them. "You wanted to protect me."

He trusted her too. She could feel that in him and knew in her heart that this was a huge step for him, that after everything he had suffered, placing his faith in a human had been difficult but he had been willing to take the risk for her.

"I would have told you." Those husky low spoken words had her eyes lifting to meet his again. "About me. I was coming to tell you... something... never mind."

She would mind, and he was going to have to live with that.

"What? You were going to tell me what?" She shifted her hand from his chest to his cheek, ran her fingers along the strong line of his jaw, his scruff tickling her fingertips, and tipped his chin up when he lowered his eyes, making him look at her. "You can tell me, Rath. You weren't coming to tell me you could transform into a cougar... you were coming to tell me something else."

Something she could see was important to him.

"I wanted to ask you..." He blew out his breath. "I was going to ask you to stay."

Her heart thumped at that and the sincerity in his eyes, the deep desire she could feel in him and knew stemmed from his need for her to remain here with him.

She wrestled with herself as she looked at him, as his feelings trickled through her, and she replayed everything that had happened, not just the fight with Alexander this time but everything that had come before it too. She sifted through her feelings, did her best to purge the lingering fear and all her doubts, and look at him with clear eyes, and an unclouded heart.

"I'll stay... until you're healed." She cursed herself for adding that when a flicker of disappointment crossed his face, hurt she had wanted to see so she could know his true feelings, what he really desired and how strongly he wanted it. It was cruel of her, but she needed to know, because this was a huge step for her too. "Or longer... if you'll let me stay."

He reached up with his right hand, tunnelled his fingers through her chestnut waves and clasped the nape of her neck. She leaned forwards when he applied the barest hint of pressure, bringing her forehead down against his. He held her there, his eyes closed, his breathing steady, his grip strong on her nape.

"I'd like that."

She went to smile, but it faltered when he continued.

"But there's one thing you need to know if you're going to stay."

A chill went down her spine, and she wanted to draw back so she could see him, but he clutched her tighter, refusing to let her move.

His words washed over her, stole her breath and birthed a thousand questions that clamoured in her mind.

"You're my fated one, and if you stay, I'll want to claim you as my mate."

CHAPTER 15

In the rankings of toughest conversations, the one Rath was about to have with Ivy was going to hit the top spot.

She pulled away from him and stared at him, her hazel eyes enormous and unblinking.

Maybe he should have waited to break it to her after she had become more accustomed to the knowledge of what he was, but with the gathering drawing closer, and the chances of unmated males arriving at Cougar Creek in the next twenty-four hours high, he couldn't wait.

She had to know now what she was getting into, because then she would understand why he had to make her leave.

At least for a few weeks, until the gathering was over.

She could come back then, when it was safe for her and her presence wouldn't make him want to fight every eligible male in the area, his brothers included.

Gods, he hoped she understood.

And he hoped she would come back to him.

"What does that mean?" she whispered.

He sat up, grimaced as his shoulder pulled tight and stung, sending fire sweeping down his side and his arm, and tried to figure out where to start.

"All shifter species, we have fated mates. They're special, rare... a person made for them." It was a poor start judging by the way she frowned at him.

"Like a soul mate?" The confused crinkle to her brow was adorable, made him want to sweep her up into his arms and kiss her.

Rath held himself back, forced himself to remain where he was and give her space, because he could see that she needed it. Everything that had happened today had come as a shock to her, and she was still processing it, and now he was adding to her burden, giving her even more to take in and wrap her head around.

"Sort of." His parents had been fated, and gods, he wished they had sat him down and told him how to explain to someone what it was to be fated. The two of them had been cougars though, so he doubted anything they could have offered would have helped him in his case. He sighed and tried to think of a better way of putting it. "Cougars and other shifters can mate with someone of their own choosing, like a marriage. We can fall in love with anyone our heart chooses too."

Like he had fallen in love with her.

"But there's a difference when you're fated?" She straightened and her eyes grew brighter, and he could see she was already piecing things together in her mind, coming to understand his species and the role of a fated mate.

He nodded. "While we can mate with anyone, can marry whoever we like as it were, the bond we share with that person isn't as powerful as it would be with our one true mate."

She dropped her eyes to her knees and frowned. "I can see why you would view it as special."

"Like a soul mate," he offered, latching onto a familiar concept for her. "You can fall in love with anyone, but what you feel when you find your soul mate... it makes that love pale in comparison."

"Was..." The way she trailed off had him aching to cup her cheek and make her look at him.

"No. It was arranged by our parents, a good match. We came to love each other in a way, but... what I felt for her, it's nothing compared to what I feel for you." He had to push those final few words out, forcing himself to lay it all out there because he needed her to know everything before she made her decision.

And he hoped it would bring her back to him.

"Because we're fated?" She glanced up into his eyes and then away again.

"No, Ivy." He did touch her now, placed his palm to her left cheek, wanting to growl as he recalled what had happened to her and saw the side of her face bloodied again. It was clean now, revealing a cut that dashed across her cheekbone and one that darted above her temple. He smoothed his thumb across them both, his touch light, filled with his need to comfort her, to take care of her. "In part, what I feel for you stems from the fact you're my true mate, but only in part. This feeling inside me... it would have been there even if you weren't my fated one."

She looked relieved to hear that, her eyes leaping to his, soft with a hint of affection that he could feel in her. "So what I feel... it's real?"

Gods, that hit him hard.

Was she saying she loved him too?

He swallowed to wet his suddenly parched throat and nodded. "I know it's a lot to take in, and I'm not expecting you to understand it all right now, or give me an answer, but I needed you to know before you..."

His cougar side snarled, bashed against the cage of his human form and had fur rippling over his skin, tearing a gasp from Ivy as her eyes darted down to his bare chest.

He couldn't bring himself to say it.

He didn't want her to leave.

"Before I what, Rath?" The way she said that, all softness and light, gently coaxing him into telling her, tore at him.

She wasn't going to understand. He would lose her if he sent her away. She would never come back. He would never see her again. It would kill him.

Those thoughts rattled through his mind at a million miles per hour, repeated over and over again as he struggled against his instincts, the fierce need to make her stay whatever the cost.

She could stay if they mated.

He just had to convince her to go through with it.

His canines lengthened in response to that, cock going painfully tight in readiness as images of sinking his fangs into the nape of her neck and claiming her rushed across his eyes, goading him into doing it.

"I don't want..." he bit out and snarled as he wrestled with himself, battled the instincts that screamed at him to claim her now before she slipped his grasp, and managed to subdue them. "You have to go."

She paused halfway through reaching for him, and her hand shook in the air between them, her hurt going through him.

Fuck, he had meant to do this more gently, in a way that wouldn't wound her, but his words had come out clipped and harsh, brutal.

"Other males are coming." His face crumpled as he looked at her and saw the pain in her eyes, agony that told him she didn't understand.

"But you want me to stay," she said, shaking her head. "You told me you want me to stay."

"I do." He moved onto his knees and grasped her shoulders in both hands, the thought of her leaving ripping him to shreds. "Gods, I do, Ivy...

but the males are coming for a gathering, to tend to the females who are needing, and if you're here…"

He lowered his head, clung to her shoulders and trembled as the need to fight for her rose to the fore, pushed him to do it now, his instincts singling out the one eligible male in the vicinity.

Storm.

He gritted his teeth. Storm wasn't a threat to him, or a rival. He was his brother. His own flesh and blood, and he knew what Ivy was to him.

He had no reason to fight him.

"If you're around those males… if you're here with me… I'm going to end up fighting them," he gritted and rather than being horrified, she simply placed her hands over his wrists, smoothed them up to his hands and took hold of them.

"Because I'm your fated mate?" She didn't sound sure.

He nodded. "Because I'll view them as a threat as long as we're not mated… not bound."

"Not married." Her voice held a slight quiver. "But if we were married…"

He shook his head. "You need time, and there isn't time before the gathering."

"So you're making this decision for me?" The snap in her tone told him how happy she was about that, and he reminded himself that he was dealing with a human now, a strong and independent female, not a cougar who had been born and raised within his world, one who would have obeyed his authority as a male. "You just get to decide what's best for me?"

He was going to lose her.

"No." He locked gazes with her again. "It's what's best for both of us. It will only be a few weeks. You can go looking for spirit bears."

She scowled at him, but then her beautiful face softened and she rubbed his hands. "Come with me."

Gods, that was tempting, had him thinking about packing a bag right that minute and not looking back.

"I can't," he croaked and growled as agony rolled through him, and fur rippled over his skin again. "I want to… I do… but my bloodline has a duty during the gathering. After Archangel attacked and we drove them back, defeated them, we vowed to protect the pride."

Her shoulders slumped beneath his hands.

"Ivy... I don't want to do this." He palmed her arms, silently begged her to look at him again as she lowered her eyes and closed up, leaving him cold.

"So don't do it."

Fuck, if only it was that simple. He had to do something, and it was tearing him apart but the path he had chosen was the right one, the only one that satisfied his deep need to keep her safe, to protect her from anything, including himself.

Forcing a bond upon her just so she could stay during the gathering wasn't something he could do.

"It will only be a few weeks, and it'll be good for you, will let you think everything over." His words sounded hollow in his ears, held a fragment of the pain beating in his heart, and he hated them, despised himself for what he was doing even when he knew it was necessary. "As soon as the gathering is over, I'll let you know, and you can come back."

She smiled tightly.

Pushed to her feet.

Left him cold as she said, "You're right. Of course, you're right. I need space."

"Ivy." He reached for her, but she backed off a step.

When the cabin door opened, she made a break for it, pushing past his brother.

Storm watched her go, one sandy eyebrow hiking up, and then sighed as he looked down at Rath and said the words that were already going through his mind.

"You really fucked up this time."

CHAPTER 16

Rath watched Ivy from the deck of his cabin, tracking her as she moved along the bank of the river, keeping away from the cabin where Ember lounged on the deck and away from Storm as he worked on another of the cabins closer to Rath's one, on the right of the clearing. She glanced at the grass from time to time, eyes drawn to the torn up earth where the fight had taken place.

The helicopter had been removed yesterday, broken down into parts and flown away by a bear shifter who had owed him a favour.

Storm had dealt with the bodies while Rath had been out, recovering from his makeshift surgery, and his brother had been guarding Gabriella ever since, keeping watch over their captive in his own cabin.

Rath could only hope for her sake that she wasn't involved in Archangel. Ivy had vouched for her apparently, but Storm wasn't convinced that they could trust the female, and neither was Rath.

Had Archangel sent her and her brother after them?

Many of the reports he'd heard about the hunter organisation in the last few decades had pointed towards them becoming more benevolent, targeting only non-humans that were a threat to humankind.

But then, there were the reports of attacks on shifter communities, ones that eventually trickled through the grapevine between species to reach him. Those reports had been coming more frequently recently, and he had the sinking feeling Archangel were going back to viewing all non-humans as a threat that needed eradicating.

Which meant they were a threat that needed eradicating.

He wouldn't let them harm his kin, or any of the other shifter species who called his part of Canada home.

Gods, he hoped that Alexander had been acting alone, out of a need for revenge, not under orders from Archangel. Even if that was the case, everyone at the creek was going to be jumpy for a while, convinced Alexander had revealed their location to Archangel and the hunter organisation would come looking for them.

The thought of his kin coming under attack again sickened Rath, had him afraid for Ivy, and for his brothers.

He needed to question Gabriella, but taking care of things with Ivy came first.

He sighed, a long slow one that fogged in the early morning air, and tried to ignore the persistent twitch of his instincts that said a male would arrive soon. He had delayed Ivy's departure for his own selfish purpose, unable to let her go while she was mad at him, liable to never return.

Storm strode out of the woods to his right, looked his way and shook his head as he slung a belt of tools over his shoulder, and kept walking, heading towards his own cabin deep in the woods to Rath's left.

He didn't need his brother constantly reminding him that he had messed things up.

Ivy was doing that enough already.

It had been two days since he had told her that she had to leave. Two days of her giving him the cold shoulder, keeping her distance from sunrise to sunset. Two days of sheer torture.

She had barely spoken a word to him, other than the occasional reminder that she needed her space.

The only thing keeping him sane was the fact she hadn't left yet, had slept each night in his arms, had even kissed him once or twice when she had thought he was sleeping.

Sleeping?

He chuckled mirthlessly at that. As if he could sleep when he knew she would be gone soon. He had spent every minute, every second of the night, awake and aware of her, watching her as she slept, absorbing every moment with her and letting none slip past him in case they were his last hours with her and all he would have to see him through the long, lonely centuries ahead of him.

He was a wreck now, close to sixty hours without sleep taking its toll on him together with the wound in his right shoulder that was still tender, was healing but hurt if he moved it too much.

Ivy's shoulders shifted beneath the dark blue fleece he had lent her as she stared down at her camera, and he could feel her hurt, and how desperately she wanted the bears to appear. She wanted them to distract her from her sombre thoughts, ones that were causing her pain.

He was causing her pain.

Gods, could he really do this?

Storm crossed the clearing again, tossed him another black look that called him a fucking idiot and strode into the woods, heading back to the cabin he was repairing. Ivy wasn't the only one giving him the cold shoulder. Storm had done his damnedest to convince him to keep Ivy around and take the leap by mating with her. His brother might live in one of the cities, but he clearly didn't have a clue about humans and how they worked.

Ivy needed time to get her head straight, because the decision he was asking her to make was one that would impact her life, changing it irreversibly.

Forever.

He couldn't rush her into it.

He couldn't.

That sensation that a male was drawing closer went through him again and propelled him into action.

He stepped off the deck and strode to meet Ivy where she was now walking towards him, her camera put away in her pack.

Fuck, this was going to hurt.

But it had to be done.

He couldn't have her around unmated males, would need to fight them, perceiving them as a threat that wanted to take his female from him even if they weren't interested in her. He wouldn't be able to stop himself from attacking them to drive them away and assert his dominance over them.

Ivy stopped as he neared her, lowered her pack and set it down on the grass, and straightened, facing him.

He sucked down a deep breath and prepared himself as he halted in front of her.

She twisted the front of his long-sleeved black t-shirt into her right fist, dragged him towards her and seized his lips in a kiss that seared him, set fire to his blood and had him forgetting the reason he had come to her, replacing it with a need that demanded he satisfy it.

Satisfy her.

She moaned into his mouth as her tongue tangled with his, stoking that need into an inferno that burned away his control, and he swallowed her sweet groan of pleasure as he banded his left arm around her, hauled her up against his chest and pinned her there as he kissed her.

Her hands skimmed over his shoulders and he shivered as she teased the nape of his neck, stroking her fingers over it, sending an achy hot wave of tingles down his spine that tore a growl from his lips and had him kissing her harder.

A need to dominate her flooded him.

He pushed back against it, set her down and stepped back, distancing himself before it overwhelmed him. "What are you doing?"

She grabbed him and kissed him again, stoking the flames that he had just convinced to go down, so they blazed through him again, threatening to rip all control from him.

Rath seized her arms and shoved her back.

Before she could kiss him again, he picked up her pack and grabbed her hand and tugged her towards the woods.

"It's time for you to leave, just for a while."

She twisted free of his grip. "No."

He arched an eyebrow and looked over his shoulder at her. "No?"

She shook her head. "I'm not leaving."

He sighed, prayed to his ancestors for the strength to do this, and reached for her hand again. "You need to leave. There are males coming."

She smacked his hand away and stood her ground. "I'm not leaving. I've thought it over, and you know what? You don't get to make decisions for me."

Reckless female.

He growled as he came to face her, but she didn't cower, just tipped her chin up and glared at him, resolve flashing in her hazel eyes.

"If you don't leave, I won't be able to stop myself from fighting every fucking male who comes," he snarled and advanced on her, closing the gap between them until his chest bumped hers and she had to tilt her head back to keep her steely eyes locked on his. "I'll fucking kill them all just for being near you, Ivy."

"No, you won't," she whispered, and she sounded so sure of herself that he wanted to scoff, but her next words froze him in place. "Not if I'm your mate, bound to you."

"What are you saying?" His eyes searched hers, darted between them so rapidly he got dizzy.

Or maybe that was just the shock of her telling him something that had to be fucking impossible, a mistake on his part, a misinterpretation of her words, although he wasn't sure how he could misunderstand them.

She made herself clear by tiptoeing, wrapping her right hand around the nape of his neck and pulling him down for another searing kiss.

She breathed against his lips, "I'm saying I want to mate with you."

Rath swept her up into his arms and kissed her, deeper this time, harder than before, unable to hold back as the thought of what she wanted rang through him, and he felt it in her blood, echoing in his veins, and found only certainty in her feelings.

Yet he still broke away from her lips and panted against them, "You're sure?"

He had told her what it would mean, had spelled out every detail for her over the past couple of days, letting her know everything that would happen if she chose to mate with him—that he would need to bite her nape while he made love with her, and that bite would join them forever, increasing her lifespan in the process.

He had told her everything in the hope it would make her do as he wanted and leave so she could think it over.

He hadn't expected her to hit him with an answer just two days later.

"I'm sure." Her steady voice and feelings backed up those words.

Rath couldn't stop himself from pulling her back against him and claiming her lips, kissing her so hard he feared he was going to end up hurting her. When she wrapped her arms around his neck, swept her tongue across his lips, and pressed inside, brushing his sensitive canines, he snapped.

She squeaked as he swept her up into his arms, cradling her against his chest, his right arm tucked beneath her knees and his left around her back.

"Your shoulder." She pressed against him but he refused to release her, only growled as her palms scalded his chest through his t-shirt and made him ache to feel them on his bare flesh.

When he reached the cabin, he kicked the door shut and carried her up to his bedroom, into the dark.

He set her down on the bed and stared at her, his heart labouring, chest heaving, body and soul screaming to claim her.

He forced himself to say, "You're sure that you're sure?"

She hit him with a dazzling smile. "I'm very sure that I'm sure. I don't want to go away, Rath... I don't want to leave this place. It feels like home... because you're here. I don't want to leave you. I didn't come here looking for this, but I'm damned glad that I found it... that I found you."

Gods, he loved her.

He snaked his arm around her waist and kissed her hard, showing her that he felt the same way, that she had become his everything, was vital to him now, and he couldn't bear the thought of being apart from her either.

Without her in it, his territory would feel empty, as hollow as his heart would be without her.

She was his home.

She was also a female possessed. He broke the kiss and looked down at her hands as they tugged his t-shirt up, wanted to grin as she hastily shoved it over his chest. A flicker of determination crossed her pretty face as she pulled it over his left arm and then her expression softened, gentling as she carefully eased it down and off his right one.

Her fingers fluttered over the bandage on his right shoulder, and he could feel she wanted to mention it, so he silenced her by pulling her fleece off quickly followed by her t-shirt. He tossed them aside and his boots followed them.

Ivy tugged her own boots off and stood, and he stilled and stared as she shimmied out of her dark charcoal hiking trousers, revealing her legs. She blushed when she caught him watching her, and then pulled down a deep breath and reached behind herself, and his own breath hitched as she unhooked her black bra and let it slide down her arms, freeing her breasts.

His already hard length shot harder at the sight of her dusky tipped full breasts and the way her nipples beaded in the cooler air, calling to him.

He growled, grabbed her around the waist and fell onto the bed with her, landing between her thighs, his chest against her stomach. She moaned, the sound music to his ears as she pushed her fingers into his hair and twisted it into her fist as he swirled his tongue around one sweet bud and sucked.

She wriggled beneath him, her breaths coming faster, and he could sense her desire mounting as she tipped her head back into the mattress. A strained moan left her lips and she arched her chest up, pressing her breasts into his face. He groaned and moved to her other breast, teasing it with his tongue as he teased her other damp nipple with his fingers, aching with a need to hear her moan again, to hear the pleasure he gave to her.

"Rath," she breathed and he shuddered, his body quaking against hers as fire swept through him, a thousand hot needles stabbing down his spine to his balls.

Gods, he wanted her.

He needed to claim her.

It pounded inside him, primal and fierce, a drumming need that he could only obey, one that hijacked control of him and had him seizing her hips and flipping her onto her front. He pulled her hips up off the mattress, tearing a delicious gasp from her, and licked her through her damp black underwear. The taste of her had him growing harder, that ache growing fiercer, and he pressed his tongue in deeper, needing more of her.

When she moved, bringing her hands to her hips, he growled and rose off her, grabbed her by the nape of her neck and pinned her to the bed. He groaned as her heat pressed against his aching shaft and he stared down at her, her submissive position stoking the inferno inside him.

She moaned as he rocked forwards, pressing his cock against her.

It wasn't enough.

He released her neck and gripped her panties, pushed them down to her knees to expose her, and groaned as he stroked her, felt how wet she was and drank down her breathless groan as she trembled.

"Gods, I need you, Ivy," he husked, and a blush climbed her cheeks as she turned her head to one side so she could see him.

He fumbled with his trousers, tore the fly open and released himself, and her eyes darkened with need as he stroked a hand down his cock, revealing the crown. That need ran in his veins, commanded him to satisfy it, to give her what she desired from the bottom of her heart.

A mating.

He had wanted to taste her, wanted to tease her to a climax before making love to her, but the passion that drenched her eyes and her feelings had him burning too hot for her, needing to be inside her now to satisfy her and himself.

He fisted his cock again, looked at it as he eased it down the seam of her backside and into her' folds, and lifted his eyes to lock with hers as he edged inside her slick heat.

His heart thundered in time with hers as it filled his ears, as he sank deeper into her and saw in her eyes every drop of the pleasure he could feel flowing through her as he joined them. He looked down at his cock again and loosed the low feral snarl that rolled up his throat as he disappeared into her, filling her.

"Fuck," he muttered, and swore that one day, they were going to do things gently, that it wasn't always going to be frantic and fast between them.

One day.

The way she wriggled, pressing back against him to drive his cock deeper into her, her eyes dark with need, calling to him, said that day wasn't today.

He grabbed her hips, pulled out of her and drove back in, a deep thrust that had her rocking forwards when their bodies met. He groaned and shuddered as his balls brushed her and she clenched around him, pushing him to the edge.

Rath leaned over her, reached beneath her with his left hand as he gripped her hip with his right, and fondled her breast as he pumped into her, each stroke of his cock sending a thrill shooting through him, a sweep of tingles that hit him from the blunt head to his balls, and back again.

She moaned and gripped the bedclothes, twisting them into her fists, and damn, the sight of her undid him, gave him that shove he needed to propel him over the edge.

He clutched her breast, pulled her up so her back was flush against his chest, and pinned her there as he angled his body lower and thrust into her, making her bounce in his arms with each powerful plunge of his cock into her heat. She moaned and tipped her head back, rubbed her hand over his hair and captured his cheek.

He groaned as she twisted her head and kissed him, lost himself in her as her tongue teased his and each breathless sigh she loosed drove him on, had him pumping deeper and harder, a slave to the primal need to satisfy her.

To mate and bind himself to her.

His canines elongated, and he shuddered as she teased them with her tongue, no trace of fear in her as she explored them.

He wasn't sure he could take much more.

He dropped his left hand to her thighs, swallowed her gasp as he teased her flesh as he plunged into her, the need for her to find release warring with a need to find one of his own by sinking his fangs into her nape.

He growled and broke the kiss, twisted her chestnut hair into his right fist and dropped his lips to her neck. Her moan sent a shiver through him, one that lit up his blood and had him thrusting faster, deeper, stroking her harder between her thighs. She arched forwards and he shook as she tightened around him, and his fangs itched, the need to bite her, to claim her, overwhelming him.

He swept his tongue over the back of her neck.

Buried his fangs deep.

She cried out, her hoarse shout filling his ears as she jerked in his arms, quivered and trembled so violently he struggled to keep hold of her. He growled against her nape as her blood hit his tongue, had stars exploding across his vision and his head spinning as release blazed through him. He grunted as his body kicked hard, cock throbbing wildly inside her, each jet of his seed tearing another animalistic sound from his throat, and an answering moan from her. Her bliss washed through him, mingled with his own to heighten it, and he clung to her as he spent himself inside her, sipped on her blood and felt the connection between them bloom.

Her feelings grew clearer, crystalizing in his mind and his heart, so he could pick out every emotion, right down to the love that burned in her heart as he held her on him and convinced himself to release her neck.

He swept his tongue across it to steal her pain away and offer a silent apology for hurting her.

When her trembling ceased, and he felt strong enough to move again, he twisted her in his arms so she was facing him and stretched out on the bed with her, holding her tucked against his chest. Her breathing slowed, her heart calming again, but the warmth and bliss he could feel in her lingered, seemed to grow stronger as she nestled closer to him.

She lifted her head and he gazed down at her, struggling to believe that she was his mate now.

His forever.

She tilted her head back and kissed him, and he held her closer, made a new vow as he clutched her to him and drifted with her in the haze of their shared happiness.

He would protect her, from now until the end of eternity. He would allow nothing to happen to her, would keep her safe and at his side. He would love her more every day, and would do all in his power to make her happy.

Because she had given him everything.

She had blessed him with her love.

She had accepted him and his world, and bravely stepped into it so they could be together.

She had made him believe in forever again.

And that forever started now.

The End

**Read on for a preview of the other books in the
Cougar Creek Mates Series!**

CAPTURED BY HER COUGAR

Gabriella glared at the black log burner set against the wooden wall of the small cabin, her fingers digging into her knees beyond the end of her grey pencil skirt, her shoulders rigid beneath her white blouse. Her lips compressed, jaw tensing as she listened to the infuriating silence punctuated only by the rapid but steady pounding of her heart.

He would come back.

He never left her alone for long.

She tilted her head to her left, just enough that she could see the door of the all-too-rustic house and the woods beyond the glass. Thoughts of escape pushed her to rise to her feet.

Her very *bare* feet.

The bastard had taken her shoes from her the first time she had tried to get away from him.

A sneaky tactic suited to the pig, and one he had completed with a satisfied twist to his bowed lips and a mocking sparkle in his grey eyes.

What sort of man resorted to removing her shoes so if she did manage to break free of her cage, she would be hobbled, slowed as she tried to pick her way through the dense coniferous forest that swamped the mountains in all directions?

Easy to capture again.

Gabi huffed, dragged her gaze away from the outside world, and tried to drag her thoughts away from escape but that was impossible now. Escape had been firmly on her mind for the past twelve hours, since she had come back to the world to find herself a captive. She didn't remember much about what had come before, only recalled snippets of wandering around the cabin in a stupor, shell-shocked by what she had witnessed.

She stared at the fire, not seeing the flames as they devoured the meagre supply of fuel.

She saw that man killing Alexander.

Saw Alexander attacking Ivy.

Kept hearing Alexander's words as he had forced her onto the helicopter in Calgary, telling her it was time she witnessed the truth of this world with her own eyes and saw justice dispensed.

Only when they had arrived in the godforsaken cluster of cabins in the disgusting wilderness, she hadn't seen justice.

She had seen Alexander and two hired mercenaries wielding weapons of war, armed to the teeth against men who had been leading what had looked like the picture postcard of a peaceful life before her half-brother had brought a battle to their doorstep in the name of revenge.

Men who had transformed into beautiful golden cougars before her eyes.

The door opened and she jumped, entire body tensing as her gaze whipped towards it and her heart lodging in her throat.

The man filling the doorway just looked at her in silence, handsome face devoid of emotion.

But there was a softness in his grey eyes as he gazed at her, one that was far from the look she had expected him to level on her after her last pathetic attempt to escape.

One that had ended with him growling at her and grabbing her, hauling her off her feet as if she weighed nothing and dumping her on his worn brown leather couch and telling her in a gruff deep voice not to move.

She hadn't.

Not because she was afraid of him, but because she was tired, soul-deep weary and didn't have the strength to move. She just wanted to curl up and sleep, to forget where she was and everything that had happened. She just wanted to go home, back to her family's mansion in England, to lounging by the indoor pool sipping cocktails and going clubbing with her friends.

God, things had to be dire if she wanted to go out with those vapid excuses for people.

Alexander was gone now. She had no reason to play her part anymore, to smile and please his friends and their friends, keeping them sweet so their investments kept his business afloat.

He was gone.

That still hadn't sunk in.

She stared at the brute as he ran a hand over his spiked sandy hair, combing it back. A few scars peeked out from the sleeves of his tight black t-shirt, red and raw, and she had a flash of him fighting, launching as a cougar to land on Alexander's back and bring him down.

To protect Ivy.

And his brother.

Bile rose up her throat as she saw that dark-haired man on top of Alexander, punching him. There had been so much blood. On Alexander. On him.

The man stepped into the cabin and closed the door, dragging her back to him. She studied him as he moved into the small kitchen area to the left of the door, using him to distract her from memories as he poured himself a glass of water, turned and planted his ass against the wooden counter.

Stared right back at her.

"How is the other man?" she whispered, needing to break the silence because it was pressing down on her, felt heavy on her shoulders and as if it might crush her.

His lips twisted in a sneer. "What do you care? Or do you want to know my brother is dead? Like yours."

She scowled at him for that.

She had never been close to Alexander, but he was her brother.

Had been her brother.

Her eyes burned, but she didn't have any tears left for him, felt dried up inside, a little hollow and numb, and now that the shock was wearing off, she felt something else too. She felt... relieved.

Was that wrong of her?

Alexander hadn't been the easiest man to live with, had resented her from the moment she had been born, as if he had blamed her for the fact his mother had remarried after losing his father. He had always made it painfully clear that her life of luxury came from his father's money too, had made snide remarks about how her father was weak and pathetic, unworthy to bear the name of his family.

A name his mother had insisted on keeping when she had remarried.

Lord.

It suited Alexander, because he acted just like one, all entitled and pompous.

Had suited Alexander.

Maybe it suited her too, because hadn't she acted the same way? Didn't she love her life of luxury and leisure?

"How is Ivy?" She wouldn't let him get away with refusing to answer that question. "I want to know how Ivy is. She was hurt."

The bastard just regarded her with cold grey eyes, making it clear she wasn't going to get anything out of him.

Gabi shot to her feet. "I have a right to know. Ivy is my friend. I was the one who arranged for her funding. I've known her longer than you and I want to know how she is! Is she a captive here too? Is that what you all do? You capture women and... and..."

She couldn't bring herself to say it.

The man's face darkened, as if he didn't like the accusation she was hurling at him either, and then calmly set the glass down and pushed away from the kitchen counter. He rounded the brown leather couch, advancing on her, long black jeans-clad legs devouring the short distance.

She stood her ground on trembling legs, her heart hammering against her ribs.

He stopped close to her, towering over her. She barely reached his broad shoulders, had to tip her head back to keep glaring at him. His eyes shifted, growing more golden as he stared down at her.

"I have a right to know." Those words came out unsteady, trembled on her lips as she faltered, fear getting the better of her. More powerful men than this one had tried to intimidate her and had failed. She wasn't going to let him win. She wasn't going to be cowed by some country brute, no matter how much stronger he was than her. She clenched her fists and narrowed her eyes on him. "Tell me how Ivy is."

He responded by seizing her right upper arm in a bruising grip and she leaned back, grimacing as she tried to wriggle free of his iron grasp. When he shoved past her and tugged her with him, her eyes widened and she shook her head.

He was taking her towards the bedroom.

His voice was a low growl as he uttered, "You gave up all your rights when you invaded our territory."

Gabi shook her head faster and frantically clawed at his hand, leaving red marks on his golden skin as she desperately tried to prise his fingers off her. Her heart went wild, thundering as fear pounded through her veins.

"Please," she whispered, her eyebrows furrowing as she looked at the back of his head and leaned away from him, trying to use her slender weight to slow him down.

He yanked her forwards and shoved her into the bedroom.

Her knees hit the bed and she fell onto it, gasped as she twisted to face him, her fear rising to swamp her and leave her quaking as cold sweat slid down her spine.

Darkness descended as the door slammed.

His gruff voice echoed through it. "You're not to leave that room. If I see you outside it, there'll be consequences you won't like."

Her eyes went wider. She had thought he had been about to deliver consequences she wouldn't like, and God, it was a relief that he hadn't. She sank against the soft bed, her breath leaving her on a long tight sigh as all her fear drained from her, leaving her shaking and weak, feeling sick to her stomach.

He moved around the other room, muttering, "Fucking humans... like I'd want one again."

She frowned at that and pushed up onto her elbows, using his words as a distraction she badly needed as she got her shaking under control. So, he had desired humans in the past? What had happened to make him hate her kind so much?

Gabi waited for him to leave, but he kept stomping around like a bear in a bad mood, making a lot of noise as he tossed dishes in the sink, proceeded to wash them, and somehow managed to make a racket as he dried the damned things. He was pissed because she had silently accused him of being the sort of man who would abuse a woman, she got that.

He didn't need to take it out on the dishes.

She eased onto her feet and looked around the dark room, but couldn't see a thing. There had to be a light somewhere. Despite the remoteness of the cabin, he had electricity. She had noticed a coffee maker in his kitchen, and other electrical items, and the living area had a lamp and an overhead light, although he hadn't used either in the time she had been locked inside her cage.

She felt her way along the wooden wall and the bed, heading away from the door. When she hit the outside wall of the cabin, she turned right, and felt her way forwards, stopped when her legs banged into a side table. She blindly explored it with her hands, sighed as she found a lamp, and fumbled with the damned thing.

The light was so bright when she found the switch and it came on that she flinched away from it.

Gabi curled her lip as she looked around the rustic room, with the blue quilt that covered the double bed and was ragged at the edges, worn from what looked like a century of use, and the rickety wooden wardrobe beyond it, and the single side table that had possibly been made by someone blind. She had never seen such awful furniture.

Still, the fact he had electricity was a godsend.

The light went out.

"For fuck's sake," the man growled from the other room and she jumped as he banged on the door. "Who said you could use the last of my electricity?"

That explained why he hadn't used the lights in the main room of the cabin the entire time she had been in it.

"It wasn't like you said I couldn't!" she snapped. "It was dark in here."

"It was dark in here," he said in a mocking, girly voice. "Fucking females. Grow a spine. You're in a room with no damned windows. It's not as if something can get in and get you!"

"*Someone* can get in and get me though," Gabi grumbled and glared in the direction of the door.

"I heard that," he snarled and her eyes widened as the sound of metal scraping drew her attention downwards and a slim shaft of light suddenly penetrated the darkness. "For that, you get locked in."

"No." She flew towards the door, slammed face first into the bed with a grunt and rolled off it, back onto her feet. She found the door handle and rattled it, twisted and turned it, and banged on the wooden panels when it refused to give. "You can't keep me in here!"

"You're like a broken record." His voice was clear through the door, and she eased back, positively jumped away from it. She had thought he had moved away again. "How about you sing me a new tune, Little Bird? Tell me about your fuck-head of a brother and your involvement in Archangel, and I'll give you a little more freedom. You want out of that bedroom, you have to sing for it, Little Bird."

Her involvement?

"I have nothing to do with Archangel." She pressed a hand to the polished wooden panel between them. "You have to believe me. I have nothing to do with them. I only helped Alexander run his business. Ask Ivy... question her. I don't doubt your brother is probably questioning her right this minute."

He scoffed and muttered, "the last thing Rath is doing right now is interrogating Ivy."

"What's that meant to mean?"

The panel creaked, as if weight had suddenly been placed on it, and she pictured him leaning against it, and the way the chiselled planes of his face would be hard, his cut muscles tensing as he crossed his arms over his broad chest.

"It means Rath wouldn't hurt a hair on Ivy's head… but you, Little Bird, if you don't start singing, my brother might just be inclined to find a way to make you… or worse… he'll leave it to me."

She backed away from the door, her heart seizing in her chest. "You're going to hurt me?"

"Only if you don't sing." His voice was a low growl, a deep rumble that rattled her with the force of his words as they hit her.

Gabi shook her head.

"How can I sing when I don't know the tune?"

CAPTURED BY HER COUGAR

In the wake of an Archangel attack on Cougar Creek, Storm is seething with a need for revenge against the hunter organisation and the key to it might be the petite blonde mortal he's locked in his cabin, one he's determined to make sing for him. Only the beauty has a fiery temperament to match his own, and the more time he spends with her, the more she stokes a fire inside him. One that fills him with a startling and undeniable need to make her sing in another way—in his arms.

Gabriella isn't going to take her captivity lying down. She's going to give the pig-headed brute holding her against her will hell until he finally believes she's innocent. He might be a cougar shifter, but she isn't afraid of him. Or at least she isn't afraid of what he is. The way he affects her, the flames that lick through her whenever they're close, terrifies her though, because the longer she's around the towering sexy-as-sin shifter, the hotter that fire blazes, and it's only a matter of time before it burns away all her restraint.

With the mating heat and the attack bringing cougars back to the creek, Gabriella is a complication Storm doesn't need, but she's one that he wants... because she might just be his one true mate.

Available now in ebook and paperback

COURTED BY HER COUGAR

Madness was sweeping Cougar Creek.

Flint had arrived four weeks ago to discover his oldest brother, Rath, had fallen in love with a human who had strayed into his territory.

A human who had turned out to be his fated female.

His one true mate.

If that hadn't been crazy enough, a week ago, a second of his brothers, Storm, had sent word that he was engaged to Gabriella, another human and one who was the half-sister of a male who had attempted to kill both Rath and Storm. A male who had been in league with Archangel, a hunter organisation that had targeted their family and their pride four decades ago too.

That battle had claimed the lives of their parents.

Flint couldn't wrap his head around the fact that Storm was now engaged to Gabriella, a woman with ties to what had happened to their parents and their pride. It was un-fucking-believable. Beyond comprehension to him. He wasn't convinced by the little mortal. She was going to have to work hard to prove she wasn't the same as her kin, working for Archangel and about to betray his brother.

He wasn't the only one at the creek who felt that way either.

Storm seemed pretty damn besotted with her though, enough to want to put a ring on it.

Literally.

Flint couldn't remember the last cougar shifter who had actually gotten hitched as well as mated with a human. He wasn't sure he had ever met one before Storm. That madness was as infectious as the other one hitting the pride, had Rath and Ivy talking about a wedding too.

He shook his head, shifted so the sole of his other worn black hiking boot rested against the rough bark of the lodgepole pine at his back, and huffed.

The whole creek had gone insane, and not in the usual good way associated with a spring gathering. This was a disturbing sort of madness, and his brothers weren't the only ones affected by it either. One of the males who had come for the gathering had ended up mating with one of the females, forming a bond between them that was the cougar shifter way of getting hitched.

Not only that.

He slid his grey gaze to his right, towards the broad river that swept around the bend at the bottom of the clearing in the dense woods, rippling over rocks and twinkling in the sunlight.

Cobalt stood by that river, a shadow in his black jeans, boots and the t-shirt that moulded to his athletic frame, a male anyone who didn't know him better could easily mistake as either menacing or a movie star depending on their gender. His brother dragged a hand over his short platinum blond hair, mussing the tufted waves that sprang back to remain perfect, and the chiselled planes of his face settled in a hard line for a moment as his gold-grey eyes narrowed on the fight, and then softened a degree again.

Flint knew why, knew him well enough to spot the subtle tells that gave away his mood.

His older brother was dangerous, but it wasn't a need to fight that had him on edge today.

Beyond him and the river, the deep green pine forest thickened as it blanketed the valley, stretching as far as the snow-capped mountains that rose into the clear blue sky, a stunning backdrop that his brother failed to notice, because he only had eyes for one beauty.

Cobalt did a poor job of hiding it too as he pretended to focus on the fight occurring between two males in the centre of the clearing, a brutal bout of delicious aggression and bloodshed over the right to be the one to ease a female in heat. Whenever Cobalt figured no one was watching him, his eyes drifted towards the spectators to single one out.

Ember.

It wasn't the first time Flint had noticed the way his second-eldest brother watched the female. Damn, it wasn't even the first pride get-together where Flint had noticed him staring after Ember with longing in his eyes.

But, it was the first spring gathering Ember was attending, here as an eligible female looking for a male.

Cobalt dragged his steel grey eyes away from her as a male approached the raven-haired beauty to speak with her. His brother shoved his hands through his pale blond hair, mussing the longer lengths on top of it in a way that screamed his frustration. Poor bastard.

Flint had a bad enough time sitting on the side lines, unable to participate in the gathering because his family were responsible for overseeing it. It was his duty to ensure things didn't get out of hand as males riled up by their instincts clashed over rights to a female, and sometimes over nothing at all. The mating fever was always strong, and he and his brothers made sure everyone was safe while they were preoccupied.

It didn't mean he was immune to the season.

So many pretty females all throwing off pheromones that had his cougar side aching to satisfy them. Damn, he would gladly satisfy more than one of them at a time if they let him.

If it was hell for him, he couldn't imagine what sort of hell it was for Cobalt, forced to endure watching males approaching a female he longed for and unable to do anything about it.

The fight finally ended with one of the males on his backside on the grass in the clearing, breathing hard as he yielded, his bare back straining beneath all the blood that covered him. His opponent hadn't fared much better, bore claw wounds that streamed crimson, but it didn't stop him from seizing hold of the female he had won the right to satisfy and whisking her away to his cabin.

Lucky bastard.

Flint would give his left nut to be able to take part in the fights, and not only because he wanted a good fuck as much as the next male right now, was wound up by all the females and ached to give them what they needed. He would have given his nut in order to just fight.

Sure, he got to bash heads together when the males broke out into battles that weren't over a female, their hormones cranking up their aggressive nature and making them volatile, easily goaded into a brawl. It wasn't the same as being able to go all out though. He had to hold back and fight to break them up, and while he roughed them up a little for being a pain in his ass, it just didn't give him the same thrill as he got whenever he really let loose.

Which didn't happen often these days.

His tour guide company up north where the Rockies gave way to rolling hills and endless plains kept him busy most of the year, from the moment the bears and wildlife emerged in spring through to the fall. In the winter, he headed west, to a small town on the coast that was occupied by shifters of various species.

Bears included.

He got to let loose a little then, whenever the bears rose to the bait or whenever they were itching for a fight too. They went easy on him though. Probably because he hired a few of them to stand in as real-life bears for the humans coming to his cabins to see the animals. Sometimes, actual bears were hard to come by, waking later in the year than the tourist season started or going into hibernation earlier than it ended. Sometimes, it paid to know a few grizzly shifters who were willing to play the role of their animal counterpart for some fast cash.

Thinking about the small group of cabins he owned had his thoughts turning to his own home there, a well-appointed lodge that was larger than the others dotted around his extensive land. It was far more sumptuous too, had every comfort he needed. From there, his mind leaped to all the tours groups he'd had to leave in the hands of his guides so he could attend the gathering as required.

Tour groups that he knew contained more than one human female who happened to be single.

Gods, he loved single human females in tour groups.

They were there for adventure, and a lot of the time, that adventure included a little real-life holiday romance when they set eyes on him. His lips curved into a grin as he thought about all the females he had indulged, letting them flirt their way into his cabin and into his arms for a few passionate nights before they left with a promise to stay in touch.

They never did.

Which was just fine with him.

He liked things uncomplicated.

He groaned and tugged his black hiking trousers away from his groin as his cock got the wrong idea, the combination of all the pheromones flying around the creek and memories of all the females he had bedded up north deadly to his self-control. He pushed them out of his head and tried to focus on other things.

It wasn't difficult when a male broke cover to his left, stepping from the trees into the clearing. He nodded to the older male, a burly brunet with a scar on his neck and a heavy pack on his back.

"You can set up on the other side of the clearing if you don't have company to bunk with." Flint pointed towards the woods opposite them, where a few cabins were visible through the trees, together with some colourful tents.

The male nodded and headed in that direction, and Flint watched him go with a frown.

Normally by now, everyone in the pride who intended to participate in the gathering had reached Cougar Creek, but each day saw more people arrive. He couldn't remember the last time his kin had resorted to camping in order to attend, or the last time there had been so many of them at the creek.

He wasn't sure whether it was because they were feeling the mating heat, or because they were curious about seeing Rath's new mate, or because of the incident with Gabriella's half-brother.

That had everyone twitchy still.

Flint glanced off to his left, up the clearing to Rath's cabin where it nestled amongst the trees at the top of the swath of green.

Rath was all smiles as he spoke with Ivy, his beautiful curvy brunette, on the deck of the log cabin. His hands clutched her hips through her pale charcoal trousers, his body pressed so close to hers that the dark green fleece he had paired with his jeans blended with her t-shirt. Flint wasn't sure his brother could get closer to her while they were clothed.

Rath's attention was all hers as she talked to him. *Besotted.* Definitely infected by the madness. His brother practically melted as she tiptoed and stroked fingers through his thick dark hair, feathered them down his neck and lured him to her for a kiss. He tangled his hands in her chestnut waves at her nape, holding her to him as he kissed her hard.

For a moment, it looked as if he was going to be whisking her away for some afternoon delight, but then his broad shoulders heaved on a sigh and he reluctantly released his mate. She said something, and he nodded and stepped off the deck.

Heading in Flint's direction.

He waited for his brother to reach him, his focus split between the crowd of cougars as it dispersed, someone helping the loser back to his cabin, and the woods that embraced the creek on all sides. It was a beautiful place, rimmed with mountains that gave the pride the privacy it needed, and he was always jealous of Rath whenever he returned to the creek.

His place up north was open on most sides, with only a few mountains dotted at a distance from the cabins, and the trees were sparser. Rath had it lucky getting to look at such breathtaking scenery year round. Flint wouldn't say no to swapping places with him, taking care of the cabins and the territory for the pride, whiling away his days fishing and soaking up the beauty of the place.

Although, that would mean giving up the life of carnal luxury he had in his own territory.

He shuddered at the thought.

He could live with a little less beauty outside his cabin when he could have all the beauties he wanted inside it, warming his bed on the cold spring and fall nights.

"...do another perimeter sweep." Rath's deep growl of a voice cut into Flint's pleasing thoughts, shattering them and dragging him back to the creek.

He looked at his older brother, who raked long fingers through his rich brown hair and heaved a sigh that stretched his fleece tight across his broad chest. Flint's own build was a touch slimmer, and he never had managed to gain the remaining two inches to match Rath's six-six height, but he had made up for that by packing on muscle, working out during the off-season to keep his strength up.

And so he looked fantastic for the ladies.

Rath's grey eyes grew golden as he looked off to his right, into the woods. "I'm feeling twitchy."

"Same here." Flint ran a glance over the cabins and trees on the other side of the clearing, and the woods that bordered the opposite bank of the river to his right. "Something doesn't feel right today."

He had put it down to the fight that had taken place, because it had been more brutal than usual, lasting longer than most battles for dominance and mating rights, which had roused a lot of the cougars from their cabins and tents to watch it play out, and had set everyone on edge as they waited to see who would emerge the victor.

But the crowd had dispersed, the green emptying, and that feeling that something wasn't quite right had persisted, niggling at him.

"I'll take a look." Flint lifted the hem of his navy shirt and hooked his thumbs in the pockets of his black hiking trousers as he pushed away from the tree.

Rath nodded and headed back up the green to his cabin.

Flint had been doing all the patrols since he had arrived. Normally, Rath did them, maintaining security for the pride during the gathering when everyone was caught up in the mating heat. The only thing his brother was sweeping this time was Ivy, up into his arms.

He shook his head as Rath pulled Ivy back against him the moment she was within reach and kissed her again. Definitely besotted. His brother couldn't keep his hands off her.

And damn, even Flint was beginning to smile whenever she appeared, because he knew Rath would be close to her in a shot, swept up in her all over again.

It was good to see his brother happy at last.

He couldn't remember the last time he had seen Rath smile so much.

Flint took one last look around the creek, at Rath where he fussed over Ivy, and Cobalt where he stood by the river clearly pining for Ember, and at the other males and females who were giving each other more than just the eye.

A sigh escaped him.

He turned on his heel, heading into the forest to start his patrol.

Yes, the world had gone mad, and he wanted no part of it, was fine with his life the way it was.

There was no damned way he was going to get caught up in whatever fever was sweeping the creek.

No way at all.

COURTED BY HER COUGAR

Madness is sweeping through Cougar Creek, and Flint wants no part of it. The fever has two of his brothers in love already, and Flint is damned if he's giving up the bachelor life to tie himself to one female, but when a perimeter sweep has him running into an exotic and enthralling beauty who rouses his instincts as a cougar shifter and a male, the hunt is on.

All Yasmin is interested in is making sure her friend, Ivy, is safe, but the alluring black-haired man with a wicked smile she meets on the path to the creek has her thinking about other things. When an incident at Cougar Creek leads to her revealing a secret, and Flint's persistence pushes her to a rash decision, her entire world is in danger of being turned upside down.

With the gathering in full swing, and males determined to prove their worth to Yasmin, Flint discovers he's not immune to the madness sweeping through the creek, because he'll do whatever it takes to claim victory and win Yasmin's heart... no matter how dangerous it is.

Available now in ebook and paperback

CRAVED BY HER COUGAR

Cobalt's heavy black boots chewed up the loose gravel at the edge of the river where he had been wearing a trench since ending his shift six hours ago, pacing relentlessly through the night as he wrestled with himself.

He should have spoken to Rath when he had arrived at Cougar Creek weeks ago, shouldn't have let it go this long without talking to his older brother. Now, it was getting harder and harder to find the right moment, or even the right words, or the damned courage to tell him what had happened, even when he needed the advice.

He needed to unburden his shoulders before he broke under the weight of it all.

It was a solid plan, and all his brother could do was shoot it down, but fuck, it was difficult just thinking about approaching Rath and laying it all out there. It had him awake most nights, restless and pacing, and he was lucky his cabin was secluded, set away from the others on its own small parcel of riverfront land, or someone would have noticed that he had gone the past four days without sleep.

Shit, someone was going to notice it soon regardless. There was only so long he could make it before one of his brothers took a look at him and finally saw just how thinly spread he was, how stretched tight and in danger of breaking.

Although, the reason he had been losing sleep might have more to do with the spring mating gathering that had called him back to Cougar Creek and a certain female who was participating for the first time.

He tried not to think about Ember, about the fact his raven-haired beauty had finally hit a century old and had matured, and how he had felt the second he had set eyes on her at the creek this time.

Cobalt tried not to think about that every damned second of the day and night, but it haunted and tormented him.

Realising she had come to attend the gathering, that males were going to fight for the right to ease her as her need to mate mounted and he was unable to be among them because of his position within the pride, had been a hard punch to the gut followed by one right in his chest that had felt as if it was going to smash his heart to pieces.

It had left him reeling, off balance and dangerous.

He had arrived at the creek in time to discover Storm, his younger brother, had gone off to fight a bear shifter, and the combination of seeing Ember at the creek looking for a male to take care of her needs and his brother in danger had sent Cobalt into a rage so deep he had come close to chasing the bear shifter when he had retreated, determined to end the bastard and uncaring whether he had to take on the male's entire pride to do it.

Only the realisation that Storm had been badly wounded had stopped him in the end, giving him something else to focus on and allowing him to pull back on the reins and regain control.

Cobalt shoved his hands through his platinum-blond wild hair and growled as he clawed at it, pivoted and began pacing back along the clearing in front of his cabin, faster now as his emotions started to get the better of him again.

He needed to fight. His muscles felt too tight, clamped on his bones, his entire body pulled as taut as a bowstring and, fuck, he was in danger of snapping.

His claws lengthened, his fangs sharpening as frustration mounted, an explosive mix of anger, shame and bitter disappointment. He snarled, lips peeling back off his teeth, and wheeled to pace back the way he had come, his strides clipped as the need to fight merged with an ache to shift.

Gods, he wanted to surrender to that soul-deep ache.

He wanted to purge every damned feeling that was boiling inside him, twisting him and pulling him apart, and let instinct take over. Shifting into his cougar form would give him that release and the relief from it all he so desperately needed.

His animal form dampened his emotions because it couldn't process them as easily as his human side so it suppressed them instead. His messy feelings would fade into the background if he remained as a cougar for long enough as his instincts rose to swamp him.

In that form, he obeyed a more basic and uncomplicated set of needs.

Fight. Feed. Fuck. Survive.

It was all that mattered when he was running as a cougar, and it was tempting to let it sweep over him, but it was dangerous too.

Those instincts were liable to send him straight to Ember.

He wanted to fight for her, as the other males could, and, sweet gods almighty, he needed to ease her needs, ached to give her the relief he could feel she desperately needed. Whenever he was close to her, it drummed in his blood and drove him to do something, whatever it took to ensure that she found the release from her instincts, from the mating heat that had brought her to Cougar Creek.

Cobalt tried to push her out of his head, but need flared inside him, made him want to claw his own damned skin off as he twitched restlessly, body primed for the delicate, beautiful female who had caught his eye two decades ago and had been on his mind ever since.

In his heart.

The sun crept higher, breaking the tops of the mountains as he turned away from the creek and paced back towards the other side of his small territory. It chased the crisp coolness from the morning air and from his arms, making him aware of how cold he had gotten in just his black t-shirt and jeans.

Cobalt slowed his step to bask in the light, letting it warm him and wash over him, wishing it would carry away all his troubles as it used to whenever he had bathed in it when he was a kid.

The mist swirled as the air heated, rippling over the surface of the shallow broad river to his right and snaking around his ankles.

He stared at the horizon and drew down a slow, deep breath of the cold air. Narrowed his focus to that distant point where jagged snow-capped mountains met the sky and let everything else fall away from his shoulders, until they felt lighter again.

He couldn't let this go on any longer.

He would go mad if he did.

With Ember's presence pushing at his restraint, cranking him tight with emotions that were tearing him apart and instincts that were making him volatile, he needed all of his focus to control himself around her and the other males. He didn't need to be distracted by what had happened.

But Rath was always caught up in Ivy, his beautiful mate, and it pained Cobalt to see them together, so happy and swept up in each other. He couldn't even talk to Storm because his younger brother was away in England looking into his mate's half-brother's background, trying to determine whether he really had been working alone and not with

Archangel, a hunter organisation that had attacked his pride almost four decades ago.

An organisation that had taken their parents from them and had come close to taking Storm too.

Just thinking about that night had the need to fight rising again, a wild and feral urge to bloody his claws and fangs in order to protect his brothers.

Cobalt focused on the sunrise again, using it to calm that urge. It was slow to leave him, his fatigue and another night of worrying leaving him worn down and weak to it.

When it had finally flowed out of him, he looked down at his hands.

At his extended claws.

He stared at them, willing them to go away, but they refused.

Fuck.

He needed to speak with Rath.

It needed to be today.

Before he became a liability, a male not on the edge but firmly over it, one who was likely to fight over the slightest thing.

And he knew with a sickening sense of certainty that if he fought, it wouldn't end there.

He would kill.

Cold went through him, his blood icy sludge in his veins, and his stomach churned.

He growled at himself. He had let this go on long enough, couldn't put it off any longer or he would be a danger to the pride.

Cobalt twisted on his heel and marched along the riverbank, heading away from the sunrise and towards the area where most of the cabins at Cougar Creek were situated.

Ember's family's one included.

His pulse jacked up as he spotted it through the trees nearest the river. The lodgepole pines and spruces sheltered it, providing some cover for it where it stood just ten metres from the riverbank, facing onto the large swath of green that formed the main area of the creek.

Smoke curled lazily from the chimney, signalling someone was up.

His step slowed and he couldn't stop himself from glancing across at the front of the L-shaped cabin as he entered the clearing and started up the two-hundred metre stretch of grass to where his brother's cabin stood at the top of it, nestled beneath the trees.

The curtains were drawn across the small windows that flanked the door of her cabin, blocking him out. An ache started inside him, throbbed deep in his bones and had his step slowing further, until he almost stopped and surrendered to it.

He wanted to see her.

That yearning burned inside him, a need he found hard to deny. His instincts pushed him to step up onto her deck and knock on her door, to go to her. Fuck, they more than pushed him.

They demanded it.

She was his.

He knew that.

Gods, he knew it.

It blazed inside him like an eternal flame that was only growing fiercer, burned so hot he felt as if it was going to devour him sometimes, utterly destroy him unless he found a way to calm the raging flames.

There was only one way that was going to happen, and while his position as pride protector had been a blessing before, keeping the females away from him because his duty meant he couldn't participate in the gathering, it was the worst of fucking curses now that Ember was taking part for the first time.

And he couldn't.

He had never hated his duty before, but he hated it with a vengeance now.

When he and his brothers had taken it on in the wake of the Archangel attack over thirty years ago, a brutal assault that had left the pride shaken and had forced them to move to a new territory, he hadn't cared. But then, shortly after they had settled at Cougar Creek, he had set eyes on Ember for the first time.

She had been a long way off maturity, a cherub-cheeked young female who would have looked like a teen nearing twenty to any passing humans.

He had watched over her whenever she had been at the creek, and had used his position as pride protector to keep the females away from him during every gathering, and damn, she had grown into a stunning female with supple curves that set him on fire every time he looked at her.

Idiot that he was, he had wanted to give her time to reach maturity before approaching her, figuring she would make an appearance at the creek at some point and he would be there when it happened since Rath kept him up to speed on who was visiting.

He just hadn't thought her first appearance after maturing would be a damned spring gathering.

Now he was stuck on the side lines, acting as security for the pride while they were caught up in the mating heat and overseeing all the fights for dominance over females that were breaking out.

Females like Ember.

But she was his, and he needed her.

He needed to knock on that door that separated them. He needed her to open it and look at him with soft eyes, ones that told him he wasn't alone, that she ached for him too, craved him with the same ferocity as he craved her.

And he needed her to open her arms to him, because what he really needed most right now was to rest his head on her shoulder, wrap his arms around her and just hold her until he felt he was back on solid ground, everything put back in place and right again.

Gods, he needed to hold her until this pain went away, just wanted one moment with her without anyone seeing them, or judging him.

He needed her to hold him together, to lend him her strength and give him courage and hope.

Hope that she would be his and hope that his life could only get better from this point.

He scrubbed his hand over his mussed blond hair, did it so much these days he was surprised he had any left, and huffed as he pushed away from her home and forced himself to head towards Rath's one-and-a-half storey log cabin at the top of the sloping green.

He trudged up the gentle hill, the growing distance between him and Ember tearing at him, and wanted to growl when a dark-haired male emerged from the woods to his right and he caught the male looking towards the river.

Towards Ember's cabin.

The hunger in the male's pale golden eyes had Cobalt looking over his shoulder, seeking the one he was looking at.

Ember stood on the deck, dressed in dark blue jeans and a thick black sweater that hugged her curvy figure, her damp ebony hair blending into the wool as it tumbled around her shoulders. She nursed a steaming mug, gently blowing on it, her profile to him and the other male.

A male who was still staring at her.

Cobalt itched with a need to change course and close the distance between him and the male to drive him away and make it clear that Ember belonged to him. The gods only knew how he managed to stay his course, finding the strength to keep moving towards Rath's cabin instead.

He glanced at the male again before taking the step up onto the deck that stretched the length of the gable end of the log cabin, finding him still watching Ember. Maybe he could just shoo the male away before rousing his brother. It probably wouldn't take much. A flash of fangs and a growl might be enough.

If it wasn't?

He was liable to take things further in order to make sure he left, and he wasn't sure he had the strength to restrain himself and stop himself from going all out on the male. Hell, the state he was in right now, frayed and close to the end of his tether, there was a danger he would skip the flashing fangs and growling and go straight to beating the shit out of the male.

So he forced himself to rap his knuckles on Rath's door instead.

Because if Ember saw that side of him, if she witnessed the darkness he held within him, she would never want him.

He eased back on the deck and glanced up at the triangular window that sat beneath the eaves of the roof as he waited. A shadow moved across them, and then the door in front of him creaked open to reveal his older brother dressed in only a loosely buttoned pair of faded blue jeans.

Rath rubbed sleep from his grey eyes and yawned.

"What's up?" his brother murmured quietly and his eyes narrowed on him as he finally lowered his hand to press it against the doorframe. "You look like hell. You alright?"

Cobalt blew out his breath. "Can we talk?"

Rath nodded and glanced back inside, up at the loft bedroom, and then reached around the door. He yawned again as he stepped out onto the deck, a navy fleece dangling from his right hand, and Cobalt moved back a step to give him room.

"Ivy's still sleeping." Rath tugged the fleece on and scrubbed his eyes again, and Cobalt envied the bastard all over again.

Not because he had a mate this time, but because he was clearly catching some good sleep, and Cobalt was on the verge of crashing and burning. Maybe after he had unburdened his shoulders, he could hit the sack.

Although, sleeping lost its appeal when he glanced over at the male and found him still staring at Ember. He needed to be around to make sure she didn't do something foolish, like accepting one of them.

He glared at the male and shivered as a hot caress slid down his spine.

Ember.

She was looking at him.

Sweet gods, the feel of her gaze on him stoked the fire burning inside him until it was in danger of decimating his restraint.

He twisted at the waist and looked at her, unable to stop himself as her eyes lingered on him.

She glanced away, her focus shifting to the male, and something crossed her face, something he foolishly read as disgust. She turned and disappeared back inside her large cabin.

Rath slumped into one of the wooden chairs to Cobalt's right, below the kitchen window of his cabin.

"There's one of only a few females left who haven't accepted any of the males' advances," Rath said dryly as he stretched his legs out in front of him and rested his bare feet on the railing around the deck. "Or maybe it's her mother who isn't accepting them."

Cobalt grunted at that. Her mother had high standards, expected only the best for her child and had been that way since they had lost her father in the Archangel attack.

It counted Cobalt out since he was a total fuck up.

And a failure.

All of his brothers were prospering, their businesses going well, and their lives with them. Rath ran Cougar Creek and had Ivy now. Storm's security business was flourishing and now he had his fated mate too. Even Flint, his youngest brother, had found his mate and was talking about expanding the wildlife viewing company he ran in the north of Canada.

They all had their mates, a woman they loved and would be with forever if things went to plan.

Cobalt had nothing.

Hitting rock bottom hurt like a bitch, slashed deep into his pride, and he had no one to blame but himself.

"What's up with you, Cobalt? You've been more distant than usual... something's bothering you, and I'm getting a bit tired of waiting for you to come chat about it."

He had to smile at Rath for that. It was typical of his brother to give him space, even when he had noticed something was wrong. Cougars were a solitary species, the males liable to fight over the slightest thing, and Rath sticking his nose into Cobalt's business would have only made him lash out at his brother.

Cobalt parked his ass against the railing next to Rath's feet, his back to Ember and the river.

"I fucked up," he muttered, weathering Rath's curious gaze but refusing to look at him. If he was going to do this, he was doing it his way. He stared at his reflection in the window, into his own grey eyes, and spoke to himself. "Everything was going great... and maybe I got a little cocky... I figured I could handle shit, knew the damned deal was foolish but I thought I had it and it would be a breeze."

He sighed and leaned more heavily on the railing, so the wood creaked beneath his weight.

"But you didn't have it," Rath said softly and Cobalt shook his head. "You can fix it though?"

He swallowed hard and shook his head again. "It's gone. The whole damn business. Bust. Just like that. It's all gone fucking south and... and... well, there's no fixing it."

"Shit," Rath muttered and laid his hand on Cobalt's leg. "That's... I'm sorry."

He shrugged that off, because what was there to apologise for? It had been his choice, not an act of the gods or something beyond his control. He had made a mistake and he had paid for it.

"What are you going to do?" Rath eased his feet down and sat up, and Cobalt felt the full force of his brother's focus settling on him and sensed his need to do something to help him.

A need that Cobalt had been banking on.

"I was thinking," Cobalt started and looked down at his brother. This was one thing he couldn't say to his reflection. He needed Rath to see how important this was to him, because he hoped that if his brother saw it, he would give him the green light without hesitation. "Maybe I could stay... here. With Ivy around now, you're going to need help at the creek... and you're bound to want to go with her whenever she travels."

Cobalt had picked up that Ivy wasn't going to give up her career as a wildlife photographer and Rath wouldn't let his mate out of his sight. He would travel to the ends of the Earth for her, and that meant leaving the creek unattended for long periods while he travelled with her.

"I can take care of things in your absence. Keep an eye on your territory and the cabins." Cobalt scrubbed his hand over his tousled hair again and then around the back of his neck as he sweated, waiting for Rath to say something.

His cabin was on the other side of the community, away from the others because of his temperament, the side of him he couldn't quite control at times.

He hated that part of himself, the way he could be in control one moment and savage the next, attacking relentlessly, unable to stop himself. He hated it because he knew everyone at the pride was aware of it, many of them having witnessed the night it had been born in all of its horrific glory.

They all viewed him as a threat, and some of them had wanted Rath to cast him out of the pride.

Storm had fought to keep him in it, his younger brother the reason that side of Cobalt had emerged. Cobalt had been on the verge of maturity, ninety-nine years old, when Archangel had attacked the pride. Their parents had allowed him to fight because he had been strong enough, and Storm had foolishly fought too, despite being close to a decade from maturing.

When hunters had severely injured Storm, Cobalt had lost it.

Everything had been a blur after that, but Rath had filled him in on what had happened, how savage and dangerous he had turned, and how he had ripped through almost a dozen hunters in order to protect their younger brother.

Since then, everyone had viewed him as fucked up.

Now, he had proven himself worthy of that title. A fuck up of the highest order.

"Sure," Rath drawled.

Cobalt snapped himself back to his brother, stared at him as he struggled to take that single word in and make sense of it, as if it was utterly foreign to him.

"Sure?" He would have fallen on his ass if he hadn't been leaning against the railing, the shock that blasted through him on realising his brother was giving his consent, was going to allow him to stay at the creek and help out, sending his mind reeling. "Really?"

Rath nodded.

"You're right, and Ivy is keeping me pretty distracted." A grin teased his brother's lips, one that said she kept him distracted a lot and he wasn't complaining. "She wants to shoot spirit bears soon, and I will want to go with her. The thought of leaving the creek unguarded has been bothering me, so maybe this is the perfect solution. You can stay here year-round with me. Some of the cabins are getting old and need more than just repairs now too."

"I was thinking about adding metal roofing," Cobalt said and when Rath's dark eyebrows lifted, he shrugged stiffly. "It'll be better for when the snow falls, will last longer than timber shingles, and I hear it offers added protection from forest fire embers."

Ember.

His focus instantly zoomed to her cabin, his senses stretching to reach her. He needed to feel her. She was as devastating as a wildfire ember, made him burn just as fiercely, and turned his focus to ashes whenever he was around her.

"That's a good idea." Rath's voice cut into his thoughts of her and he forced himself to give his brother the whole of his attention. "It'll be a lot of work though."

"I can handle it." He could.

This was his chance to prove himself to his brother.

Maybe it was more than that. Maybe it was a shot at proving himself to the pride too.

He had never really fitted in at the creek, had never felt it was his home, but now he wanted to make a place for himself here.

He wanted to get his head on straight again and felt in the pit of his soul that this might be something he was good at and wouldn't mess up because of his problem. He would keep enough distance from Rath, would work on his own parcel of land and help around the creek, and would make a go of it here, where it was quiet and soothing.

"Measure up the cabins, start with our ones, and see what sort of prices you can get. I'll talk to the other cabin owners, but I'm sure they'll be onboard." Rath's faith in him touched Cobalt, eased the weight on his shoulders and had him eager to get going, and unable to believe he had put off talking to his brother for so long.

He should have known Rath would be understanding about it and would give him the second chance he badly needed.

He looked around the creek as the sun rose, bathing the mountains that surrounded the remote valley in warm light that turned the snow on their peaks gold and seemed to make the rich green of the forests that swathed their bases even more vivid.

He could make a home for himself here, finally settle down and plant some roots. No more wandering. It was time he stopped moving, stopped running from himself and faced things head on.

Ember was here now.

He had waited for her for so long, and sure, this wasn't how he had planned it, but he was damned if he was going to let the female he had been craving for the past two decades, a female who owned his heart and him completely, go without a fight.

His irises must have changed, glowing golden as thoughts of Ember merged with a need to fight for her, to take down any male who stood between him and her.

"The work thing the only stuff you need to talk about?" Rath eyed him closely.

Cobalt forced himself to nod.

While it felt good unburdening his heart to his brother, getting it all out there, he couldn't tell Rath the other reason he was feeling volatile, constantly on a razor's edge. That would mean confessing something he wasn't ready to tell Rath yet.

Something he had been aware of from the second he had set eyes on her all those years ago.

Ember was his fated mate.

CRAVED BY HER COUGAR

For the last twenty years, Cobalt has burned with a need of one female, a beautiful raven-haired cougar who captured his heart the moment he set eyes on her. His position as pride protector has been a blessing at past mating gatherings, keeping females away, but this time it feels like the worst of curses, because the female who has bewitched him so thoroughly is taking part for the first time and all he can do is watch as males battle for her.

As much as she hates the way her mother controls everything in her life, Ember is thankful for it as she constantly turns away suitors, unaware of the pain she's sparing Ember from with every male she rejects. Every male who isn't the gorgeous blond with darkness in his eyes and an easy smile she burns for with an intensity that scares her, awakens feelings in her that have her verging on doing something reckless. Damaged goods he might be, dangerous and unpredictable, but with every contest over her that pulls her closer to her doom, she grows more determined to follow her heart, no matter the consequences.

With every fight over the right to Ember, the tethers on Cobalt's feelings twist and threaten to snap, a torment he cannot bear and one that has him willing to risk it all, because a single kiss would make even the harshest punishment worth it. He would die for one moment with her... his fated mate.

Available now in ebook and paperback

ABOUT THE AUTHOR

Felicity Heaton is a New York Times and USA Today best-selling author who writes passionate paranormal romance books. In her books she creates detailed worlds, twisting plots, mind-blowing action, intense emotion and heart-stopping romances with leading men that vary from dark deadly vampires to sexy shape-shifters and wicked werewolves, to sinful angels and hot demons!

If you're a fan of paranormal romance authors Lara Adrian, J R Ward, Sherrilyn Kenyon, Gena Showalter, Larissa Ione and Christine Feehan then you will enjoy her books too.

If you love your angels a little dark and wicked, her best-selling Her Angel romance series is for you. If you like strong, powerful, and dark vampires then try the Vampires Realm romance series or any of her stand alone vampire romance books. If you're looking for vampire romances that are sinful, passionate and erotic then try her Vampire Erotic Theatre romance series. Or if you like hot-blooded alpha heroes who will let nothing stand in the way of them claiming their destined woman then try her Eternal Mates series. It's packed with sexy heroes in a world populated by elves, vampires, fae, demons, shifters, and more. If sexy Greek gods with incredible powers battling to save our world and their home in the Underworld are more your thing, then be sure to step into the world of Guardians of Hades.

If you have enjoyed this story, please take a moment to contact the author at **author@felicityheaton.com** or to post a review of the book online

Connect with Felicity:
Website – http://www.felicityheaton.com
Blog – http://www.felicityheaton.com/blog/
Twitter – http://twitter.com/felicityheaton
Facebook – http://www.facebook.com/felicityheaton
Goodreads – http://www.goodreads.com/felicityheaton
Mailing List – http://www.felicityheaton.com/newsletter.php

FIND OUT MORE ABOUT HER BOOKS AT:
http://www.felicityheaton.com

Made in the USA
San Bernardino, CA
27 May 2019